DEAD CEREUS

KIRA SEAMON

Paperback ISBN: 979-8-9850-9560-9

Hardcover ISBN: 979-8-9850-9562-3

To my parents: in loving memory of the magical garden of my childhood.

THE HOLLY AND THE IVY

The holly and the ivy
When they are both full grown
Of all trees that are in the wood
The holly bears the crown...

—Early 19th Century British Christmas Carol

INTERESTED IN A FREE BOOK FROM KIRA SEAMON?

Keep up to date with the latest news, upcoming releases, and free books from Author Kira Seamon by visiting her website.

https://www.kiraseamonauthor.com

CHAPTER ONE

*H*olly's eyes grew larger and larger as she scanned the newspaper article on the kitchen counter. She glanced at the microwave oven and saw that her food had completely steamed up the inside glass, indicating it would be ready in about a minute. Quickly returning her attention to the title of the article, she read: *Body Found in Prestigious Providence, Rhode Island Greenhouse Yesterday.*

Wow, I was just down there at the Botanical College of Providence's greenhouse last month for a bonsai workshop, Holly remembered. *And now they found a dead body!*

She continued reading: *Providence police have launched an investigation into the mysterious death of a college student. The college had just wrapped up a series of special workshops and lectures by famous botanist Professor W. Ogletree of the Ogletree Chocolates empire. The public was invited to attend these offerings, which brought thousands of people from all over New England to the campus over the last week. The police currently have no leads and are asking for the public's help. They have set up a tip line to call if you have any information about this case.*

"Professor Ogletree goes between our two colleges regularly!" Holly squealed under her breath. "I better cut out this article and show it to William." She efficiently clipped the article and tossed the remainder of the newspaper in the trash. Stuffing the article into her trendy small handbag, she walked over to the microwave oven to calm its incessant beeping.

As Holly bent down, she caught a quick glimpse of herself reflected in the door.

With her scholarship at Shellesby College hanging by the thinnest thread, she couldn't afford to be less than her best today. She gazed in approval at her polished look.

Her large green eyes were set off to a nice effect with soft eye shadow. A hint of blush accented her cheeks, and a pretty dark pink shade of lipstick coated her lips. She could see the top of her light brown, crushed-velvet dress in the reflection and thought she looked polished and professional. Normally, she preferred to wear jeans and a tank top, but this was the most important weekend of her school year, and she wanted to dress to impress. In her junior year as a scholarship student, prestigious Shellesby College expected her best behavior to earn her right to stay there, especially now that she was virtually on probation with Director Berkeley again.

A final glance at her reflection caused her to grimace slightly. Her curly red hair started to escape the hairspray and gel she used to tame its usual wildness. Tendrils from her updo curled around her face, and she brushed them back with an impatient hand.

Nevertheless, she was satisfied with her overall appearance today and opened the microwave door. A sweet aroma blasted her in the face, assaulting her with the most delicious-smelling, fresh-baked raspberry muffins. She had baked them herself yesterday in her dorm kitchen using berries grown in the school's garden.

Placing the muffins on a highly polished silver serving tray, she put them on the table in the middle of the room and quickly walked the length of the Visitor's Center meeting room, exiting to the outside.

She squinted into the sun as she peered at the welcome banner hanging directly over the door.

She shaded her eyes from the glare and read the words: *Morning Glory Event Today*. The door itself was encircled by a trellis with flowers growing on it. Holly had trained those morning glory flowers onto that wooden trellis and fertilized the vines heavily to encourage them to put out their large, trumpet-like flowers. These flowers heralded the arrival of some very special guests today.

The top five big-wig donors to Shellesby College from this year received an invitation to a special annual recognition event called the Morning Glory. At this event, they would be presented with their donation plaques. These permanent plaques would then be assigned to the different rare plants that their donation dollars made possible to acquire. This was where they got the "glory" for the large sums of money they donated to help the greenhouse maintain its status as one of the top five greenhouses in the world.

Holly heard a small squeak and looked down in time to see a tiny red-brown chipmunk dash by, but she had no time for Huckleberry right now.

She felt a tiny prickle of worry and apprehension slide down her spine but shrugged it off and vowed to think positively. Everything needed to be perfect today. This was the very first time Director of Horticulture, Professor Emeritus Ashton Berkeley, had entrusted her to run the Morning Glory event all by herself, and if she pulled it off, she would redeem herself in his eyes. Lively voices came up the path to the greenhouse complex, and she whirled on her heels to greet them.

"Hello, ladies and gentlemen! I'm Holly, your guide for the Morning Glory event today, and I can't tell you how grateful all of us here at the greenhouse complex are for your extremely generous donations this year. We hope you enjoy the deluxe plaque presentation we have planned for you today. Please step this way and find your seat at our table. Fresh-baked muffins and mint tea await you."

Holly held the door open, and the five wealthy alumnae and their husbands walked through and sat at the table. They loudly exclaimed in appreciation as they took in the stunning floral tablecloth, flower arrangements, and the elaborately designed name cards waiting for them on the table.

"It's always a pleasure to see you again," Heather Moore said.

"Likewise!" Holly chirped. She knew Heather was an alumna Shellesby College could count on year after year for the gigantic donations she made specifically for greenhouse upkeep and maintenance. Heather ran the National Botanical Gardens in Washington, D.C. but always cleared her calendar, without fail, for Shellesby's annual Night Lights Ball weekend. She enjoyed flying up to the college, located in the West Shire-ston suburb of Boston, Massachusetts, to attend all the festivities.

"The muffins are scrumptious. Which variety did you use for the mint tea?"

"This is a blend of our spearmint and peppermint in a one to three ratio with a tiny smidgen of our chocolate mint to round it all out. You all can see them growing there right outside our door!"

She gestured for the group to look through the giant floor-to-ceiling picture windows that lined one side of the Visitor's Center meeting room. Rows upon rows of different herbs grew there in perfect uncluttered precision.

Holly had to turn away from the group briefly to hide a smile.

Some very weird, blockbuster herbs grew in a tiny corner

on the left, but they were indistinguishable from the other herbs to an untrained eye. She had big plans for those blockbuster herbs, a super-secret mission that would be carried out at the Night Lights Ball many hours from now. She couldn't wait.

She hid her slightly mischievous smile and turned back to face the group.

"I loved tending the herb garden when I was a freshman," Heather said. "Weeding it was one of my favorite chores here."

"For us too!" a duo in their sixties chimed in. Holly smiled at the two women before one continued. "This room brings me right back forty years ago to when we took Horticulture 101. I don't believe we've met. I'm Jasmine, and this is my sister, Jessamine. I'm Class of '76, and my sister is Class of '79."

"Yes, it's great to meet you both!" Holly remembered reading up a little on these donors beforehand and found out both had gone on to Harvard Law School. Jasmine was now Massachusetts State Attorney General while Jessamine was the Mayor of Cambridge. These accomplished African-American women also sponsored different scholarships at Shellesby, including athletic scholarships.

"Well, that leaves just us," another woman said. "I'm Viola, and this is my identical sister, Violet. I'm five minutes older than her, which definitely makes me the big sister and decision-maker in our family!"

"Hold on there, V! I was just being polite and letting you get born first, so I'd say I'm the one with the manners in this family!"

Both ladies laughed. A combination of generally sunny dispositions and good face moisturizers had let the ladies age well and without too many wrinkles or frown lines. As such, they were still almost indistinguishable from each other. Holly had given up trying to figure out who was who and just called each "V."

"Now that we've taken the edge off our hunger with a muffin or two, we'd better get started because I think Professor Berkeley wants me to do a lot of decorating here in a couple of hours."

With that, Holly snatched a small muffin off the tray and stuffed the whole thing in her mouth but covered her mouth with her hand as she chewed, showing a trace of decorum.

"Please come this way," she mumbled around the muffin.

Holly held open a screen door, and the group walked into the first room of the greenhouse complex—the Desert Room.

This marked the beginning of the greenhouses: airy, metal structures interconnected and entirely created with double-paned windows. There were five main rooms with smaller student nurseries branching off from the main rooms. Tables overflowing with plants in clay pots lined the perimeter of each, and each room also boasted a special display of rare and valuable plants as a centerpiece. The plants there grew directly in the soil of the display.

The center display in each of the rooms was set off by a low one-foot tile wall that encapsulated the main display and kept it separated off the circular pathway that ringed it. Each room had a theme, and the Desert Room concerned itself with dozens of specialty cacti and other succulents. This room was kept at a significantly drier humidity than the other rooms in the complex.

"Is that her? Wow, she has grown a lot this year!" Heather exclaimed.

The group inspected the dark green vine with long, spiky leaves that had very large buds on them. The buds looked swollen with anticipation. The vine grew in a pot but had gotten so tall and spread so much it had been trained to cover an entire wall of the Desert Room and came close to the top of the very roof.

"That's her! Do you want to tell the group how you found her?"

"Indeed, I do. It's one of my favorite botanical trips ever! I was determined that this greenhouse has a choice Queen of the Night night-blooming cereus plant. These plants grow in deserts. I sponsored a multiday trip to Arizona for the College to visit the best cactus farms there, and we chose this plant for our collection."

"Tell them where you found it, Heather," Holly encouraged.

"Yes! Get this, ladies and gentlemen. I found it in Tombstone, Arizona! I led an expedition consisting of Professor Berkeley, Ivy Berkeley, and William Smith, and we visited every cactus farm in the Sonoran and Chihuahua Deserts in southeast Arizona." She paused here and shook her head in amazement at that memory. "Boy, that town is aptly named. Tombstone! I thought I'd die from the heat there. It was taxing, but the trip was worth it to find this amazing specimen. Should I tell them the story?" Heather asked, looking at Holly.

"No, don't tell them that story," Holly answered.

"Are you sure? It's a great story!"

"I hate that story," Holly replied good-naturedly with a smile.

"But it's a good story!"

"What story?" asked Viola and Violet.

"It's a story about…" Holly began.

"What? A story about *what*?" Jessamine and Jasmine asked.

"Should I just tell them the story?" Heather asked.

"I hate that story!" Holly repeated.

"What story!" everyone in the group screamed.

"Oh, nothing much. A story about…bats. That's all."

"Bats!"

"Here, I'll help you tell the story," said Heather. "So, this rather unremarkable cactus has one claim to fame. Only once per year, at night, it blooms, but it is so remarkable and fascinating that it's worth the year wait! On the night it blooms, we hold a Bloom Party, a watch party if you will. These blossoms are showstoppers! Huge blooms, easily eight to ten inches across. Pure white with yellow highlights that glow magically in the moonlight."

"So," Holly said, picking up the thread of the story, "two years ago, in my infinite wisdom, I suggested that we open our retractable roof during the Bloom Party because the air was so clear that we could see the Milky Way stars above."

"And we *did* see the Milky Way stars above," Heather confirmed. "That is, until they were blotted out of view by the black squadron of bats that flew over here from the belfry!"

The entire group gasped in unison.

"Yes!" Heather said. "Do you remember our carillon? It's the bell tower on the Academic Quad. It's a set of bells positioned high up directly under the roof of the tower."

"I'm taking Advanced Carillon this year. The carillon is played on a keyboard-like instrument that corresponds to the bells situated up by the roof. Suffice it to say, we also have a resident bat flock that lives up in that belfry," Holly said, trying to end the story.

But Heather wasn't finished and was just warming to her subject. "Now, the main pollinators of the night-blooming cereus are bats! Bats may not have great vision—ever hear the phrase 'blind as a bat?'—but they sure have an ultra-keen sense of smell! The flower is especially fragrant, and the bats smelled the blossoms and wasted no time coming to investigate!"

"Before we knew it, we had bats flying in all over the place," Holly recalled with a shudder.

"Holly got in a lot of trouble for that with Director Berkeley," Heather added.

"Yes, that's why I hate the story. In fact, let's move on before I...go batty."

Everyone laughed.

"Is she going to bloom in time for the Night Lights Ball? Her buds look so big I think they'll open any night now!" Heather asked excitedly.

"Well, William measured their circumference, and sadly, it looks like they will open just a night or two too late. It looks like they need at least three more nights until they open."

"What a shame! I always look forward to her annual bloom!"

"Yes, William thinks it's a shame too, so he's injecting the plant hourly with liquid fertilizer to see if he can speed up the process."

"William is such a diligent student! The college is so lucky to have found him!"

"So true," Holly agreed, thinking about her boyfriend.

William was twenty-six years old and going for a double doctorate at Shellesby in both horticulture and botany. He had already made discoveries in grafting techniques as a teenager and was regularly written up in *Horticultural Digest* for his groundbreaking inventions in the botanical field. A standout student, he had caught the eye of the horticulture department's director, who gave him many important assignments in the greenhouses. He had a bright future and hoped to run a major botanical garden organization himself one day.

Tall and athletic with a wicked sense of humor, he was Holly's everything, and she felt lucky he loved her. He lived close by Shellesby's campus—right across the street, in fact—within an easy five-minute walk to the greenhouses. He found a small cottage available to rent, which he called his "Cot," and she regularly stayed over with him when her busy schedule allowed.

"We better keep moving now...Before we leave, I'd like to quickly point out the old man cactus."

The old man cactus was another stunning plant. It was a tall column of pokey spines with an amazing shaggy coat of long white hairs, which are suggestive of the unkempt hair of an old man. It usually drew many gasps of admiration from visitors to the greenhouses and was a favorite of the staff and students alike.

"Well, he has more hair than I do!" Viola's husband said while ruefully rubbing his bald head. "Is this what I've come to? I'm envious of a cactus?"

"You are envious of a succulent, it's true," Viola said with a laugh.

The centerpiece of the cactus display was the huge golden barrel cactus, dominating the room as it did with its enormous spines jutting out a few inches from the main plant. Two feet across, it was a fearsome plant that was just starting to put out a couple of delicate blooms on its very top.

"Here is our golden barrel cactus. William is the legit cactus whisperer. He has never gotten a thorn in his finger in all the time he's worked here!"

"I think that's the product of wearing four pairs of gloves rather than his calming bedside manner," Heather said with a laugh.

"Violet, that cactus is less prickly than you are before you get your morning coffee!" Violet's husband joked.

"Har-har," Violet said. "I see that you are...ahem...scraping the bottom of the *barrel* with your jokes this morning, dear."

The group again laughed.

Holly pointed out that all these hardy plants needed sparse watering yet grew profusely and vigorously. She gestured to show the room was flanked on all sides by dozens of other cacti, succulents, and desert plants with small blossoms or prickly pears on them.

Walking around the large dragon tree in the middle, she said, "Ladies and gentlemen, let's keep moving. We have places to go and *trees* to see!"

Holly pushed open the far screen door, and they entered the Camellia Room. All the display rooms of the greenhouses were designed for a north/south layout, with the east side of each room having an emergency exit door as per the local building code and the west side of each room leading to the smaller rooms of the greenhouse complex. These rooms were used exclusively by the students and William. Screen doors separated each display room from the other and were also used for the west exits into the smaller rooms of the greenhouse.

The screen door gently closed behind the group, and they were treated to the angelic vision of a very large camellia tree.

As she entered the Camellia Room, Holly suddenly felt pinned to the spot with the weight of someone's gaze.

Turning her head to the right, she saw Ivy Berkeley sitting like a princess on an ornate chair next to the camellia tree while having her portrait painted by an artist who stood in front of a large easel, holding a large palette of oils.

Ivy's ice blue eyes stared daggers at her.

Holly was ready to slap a hand to her forehead in dismay.

She had forgotten that Ivy had daily portrait sessions in here before the greenhouse officially opened for the day.

Holly took a closer look at Ivy sitting so motionlessly for her portrait. Sitting so still, she appeared to Holly like a mannequin, which seemed apropos since Ivy always gave surface answers and appeared rather fake most of the time. Holly didn't remember a single spontaneous phrase she'd ever heard from Ivy. Everything she said was geared to please her father.

Holly felt her shoulders tightening up with the familiar tension she always felt with the Berkeleys, both father *and* daughter.

They descended from the original Mayflower Pilgrims and, as such, had had centuries to build their wealth. Their family also was rumored to have been related to the Carnegies and the Rockefellers. Needless to say, they were extremely well-off, and Berkeley continued the tradition of getting a portrait done of every family member once they turned twenty-one years old. Ivy's birthday was coming up soon.

Everyone grouped around the portrait and marveled at the likeness of Ivy.

"Please, don't let us keep you," said Ivy. She sat so still and tried not to move her lips lest she move out of position for the painter. She seemed like a ventriloquist as she spoke, and Holly realized she *was* like a puppet being pulled by her dominating father's strings.

Holly continued her tour. "So, this camellia tree was planted by our college's founder, and it is the only plant afforded a permanent space in the greenhouses since their inception. It is over 160 years old. We are loath to disturb this most precious and important tree, and so everything about the greenhouses was designed around it."

The group marveled at the camellia tree, which stood at least thirteen feet high with hundreds of pink and white variegated blooms. The tree was set off to best effect amidst a stone pathway and Japanese-inspired rock garden. It shared its room with many jade trees and looming Mediterranean cypress plants, large potted evergreen coniferous trees that stood as sentinels alongside the screen door that separated the Camellia Room from the Tropical Forest Room. The Camellia Room was noticeably cooler than the Desert Room, as the camellia preferred a more temperate environment.

"You wouldn't believe the amount of babying that tree gets!

William is so diligent. He even wakes up in the middle of freezing winter nights to come down to the greenhouse to take the temperature in this room. If it's too cold, he sets up space heaters around the tree to eliminate any risk of frost damage to our most special tree."

"Yes, William treats these plants and trees as if they were his children!" Heather exclaimed. "He's the best!"

"Oh, he definitely is!" Holly agreed.

"He always says, 'Where there's a Will, there's a way!' And in fact—"

"If you are quite finished, Holly," Ivy suddenly interrupted, "we'd like to continue now so I can get to class." Her voice was as cold as the icebergs in Antarctica.

Holly felt the familiar crackle of electricity in the air whenever she and Ivy had confrontations.

To be completely honest, Holly felt jealous of Ivy for her privilege and good looks. Ivy had the pretty features of a model and was tall with amazing blonde hair. Her looks, coupled with her jaw-dropping credit score, made her a rival for William's attention, and Ivy *did* try to catch his eye at every opportunity.

William remained loyal throughout Ivy's flirtations, but it grated on Holly, nevertheless.

Biting her tongue this time, Holly silently led the donors out of the room.

The group pushed through the screen door that separated this room from the next and immediately fell silent. A hush permeated the room, and the only sounds came from the fans that stayed on all the time to give proper ventilation in the greenhouse.

The group slowly looked skyward and marveled at the exotic large trees growing there.

Huge flowering trees of every description provided a kaleidoscope of colors and shapes.

Bougainvillea with large sprays of blossoms in red, orange, and yellow grew in shaggy bushes along the windows of this room in the greenhouse complex. A torch ginger grove was in the middle along with overflowing hibiscus bushes. The hibiscus was in such profusion that their large, showy blossoms intermingled with the other jungle-like plants to create a sea of tropical flora.

This display room felt as humid as a Florida afternoon in mid-July, and there were tiny swarms of gnats that could not be gotten rid of. This was the most mysterious of the rooms, as the layout of it did not give viewers an unfettered glimpse across the span of the room. Overstuffed—indeed, over-planted—with the most magnificent palms and tropical plants, it was an entire tropical jungle stuffed into a terrarium-sized space.

Heather laughed, breaking the spell, and said her glasses had fogged up from the intense humidity of the room.

"I feel like I'm on a set for the film *Jurassic Park*," Jasmine's husband said.

Holly also recovered her composure, but being awestruck was the most common reaction to the trees in the Tropical Forest Room, even for those who saw them every day.

For infrequent or new visitors, the effect was simply jaw-dropping.

This room alone earned the Shellesby College greenhouse complex the prestige of one of the top five greenhouses in the world.

"Well," Holly said after the *oohs* and *aahs* had simmered down, "unfortunately, I have another story to tell you. I might hate this story even more than the bat story, but it is integral to why you're here today."

The group waited in anticipation.

"Simply put, your donations have made this room what it

is, no more and no less. Without you, we would have faced a catastrophe. The college and I are forever in your debt."

"Can you explain the catastrophe?" Heather asked.

Holly nodded painfully.

"One of my many jobs here is to be in charge of the plant donations. Two years ago, we received a donation of a wonderful Guadalupe palm specimen. This was a mature tree, and it is, in fact, on the world's endangered list as it is native only to Guadalupe Island in Mexico. To have one in our collection was a true highlight for the greenhouse that year."

"That sounds amazing," V said. "How was it a catastrophe?"

Holly swallowed hard.

"Unbeknownst to me, there was an undetected locust egg infestation in the soil of the container in which the palm was living. These locusts hatched, and in less than twenty-four hours, they ate every single leaf of every single tree here in the Tropical Forest Room!"

The group gasped in horror as Holly pressed a hand to her heart.

"It was an unmitigated disaster! Professor Berkeley had to be sedated and hospitalized from the stress of it all."

And as luck would have it, Professor Berkeley happened to push through one of the screen doors at the far end of the room and strode forward to greet the donors.

"Did I hear the word *locusts*? Locusts, *schmocusts*! Holly, you know that I've banned that word from ever being uttered in this room!"

With an unkind look at Holly, he strode past her and stood before the donors.

"Berkeley! Good to see you, man!" Heather said.

"It's a pleasure as always." He gave her a quick embrace.

"I can't tell you how much your donations have meant to the

college and me personally. Restocking this Tropical Forest Room with these rare and exotic prize specimens of plants and trees has been the true highlight of my tenure here. Your gifts were the only thing that made such a tremendously expensive undertaking possible. As such, we have the great honor and pleasure to unveil here today your plaque, renaming the entire Tropical Forest Room the MORNING GLORY 2021 DONORS ROOM."

The group gasped again but in pleasure this time.

"We still informally call it the Tropical Forest Room," he added. "But please feast your eyes on this brand-new sign above the main door."

The group turned around and stared at the huge sign above the door, declaring the new name change.

Viola and Violet wiped away twin tears from their cheeks.

"Berkeley, it is the honor of my life to have been a part of something so special here at the greenhouse complex. We *love* this college with all our hearts, and to hear that we could help the college out in its dire time of need gives us deep satisfaction and a feeling of peace and contentment. We are so happy to help!"

A few more tears slid down two pairs of moisturized cheeks, and then they sniffed once and composed themselves.

Jasmine said, "I must express the same feelings as Viola and Violet. My sister and I are humbled that our donations could affect a purchase of this magnitude."

Berkeley beamed with pride. "I would love to stay longer, but I'm needed in about seven places at the moment. I look forward to catching up with you all much more during dinner at the Night Lights Ball!" And with that, he left the room.

"I'd like to point out our beautiful shell ginger grove to you." Holly resumed the tour and led the group to a grove of plants that had beautiful clusters of yellow and white flowers reminiscent of the shape of a shell. "As you may know, shell ginger is Shellesby College's official flower!"

The group murmured in appreciation and leaned in to smell the profuse blossoms.

"I'd also like to show you our carnivorous plants section! We even have some very toxic plants in here. You could literally kill someone in a greenhouse if they got a hold of the wrong plant!"

Just then, Professor Ogletree entered the room with campus security.

As he pushed his way past Holly, he glared momentarily at her. "Don't be so morbid. That's the last rumor this college needs."

"Oh, hello, Professor Ogletree. I hope your trip back from Providence was pleasant," said Holly, trying to put on her most dazzling smile.

"It was, but my trip was cut short because of a situation here in this greenhouse. Seems some of the nightshade plants have been taken," he said with a stern expression and a slight curl of his upper lip.

"Oh, I hadn't heard! Is there anything we can do, Professor Ogletree?"

"No, I'm sure it's just a silly prank. However, given the toxicity of the plant, until we find out who took the nightshade plants, we'll have this fenced area under guard. Gentlemen, please attend to your posts by the fence. Do not leave your guard duties unless instructed by me. Guests, I hope you enjoy the rest of your tour. If you have any questions, please don't hesitate to reach out to Ivy Berkeley. I believe she is back in the Camellia Room." With that, Professor Ogletree turned on his heel and left the greenhouse.

The guests murmured amongst themselves for a moment.

Holly suddenly recalled that article she read earlier about the dead body found in the Providence greenhouse, and a chill went down her spine. *I bet you really can kill someone in a greenhouse if you are motivated to,* Holly thought.

Shaking herself out of her increasingly anxious thoughts before they spiraled out of control, she snapped her attention back to the group.

Holly sidled away from him and pointed out the Venus flytraps in their little orange clay pots on a table lining the wall. "Here are our pitcher plants and Venus flytraps. They work by catching their prey, which are insects! The pitcher plants secrete this sticky substance in the middle of their flowers, and when ants and bugs, spiders and such, venture in… they don't venture back out again due to the stickiness! The Venus flytrap senses when a fly flies into its center and then rapidly snaps shut its two halves."

The group peered at the various carnivorous plants in admiration.

"So, these are hunter plants, if you will. They eat meat!" Viola's husband said with a gleam in his eye.

"They certainly do! And if you come over here, you will see our deadly oleander, hemlock, and where the nightshade used to be!"

"In Ancient Greece, hemlock poisoning was a common punishment for prisoners. Socrates died from it! I remember that from antiquities class when I was a sophomore," Jasmine said with authority.

"You are exactly right! That's why we keep those toxic plants fenced in so the public cannot access them. Those plants mean business, and we don't want to see anyone getting hurt here in our greenhouse!" Holly emphasized.

The group now wandered over to admire one of the most eye-catching plants. The towering white bird of paradise sprawled its huge, palm-shaped leaves over the gingers and hibiscuses that populated the mid-space of the beautiful room. This white bird of paradise emitted huge, white, elaborate blossoms that jutted out from its center.

"Wow! I saw a much smaller bird of paradise when I went

to Hawaii last year, but this gigantic specimen is magnificent! Where did this come from?" Heather asked.

"This one came from the director's expedition to Mozambique. By the way, something else I want to mention: we not only had director Berkeley go around the world to source these rare plants, but he hired local horticulturalists to accompany them when shipping them back here to us so they wouldn't be damaged. They needed delicate care along the journey. And the shipping might have been even the biggest cost of all! After all, it isn't free two-day Amazon Prime shipping!"

The group laughed.

Holly smiled, and then her smile froze on her face as she heard the tell-tale spurts of water starting to gush with jet force from the sprinklers on the roof.

Watering hoses lay on the side of the pathways in most display rooms, and most also had sprinklers that rained water down at timed intervals. This tropical jungle was liberally doused with water from the sprinklers before the greenhouses opened to visitors and again after closing.

Holly felt like she was going to faint. She had messed up again! She had forgotten to turn the sprinklers off their set timers. Usually, no one but the staff was in here so early.

"Quick, everyone, run!" Holly sprinted to the exit door of the Tropical Forest Room, but it was too late. As she held the door open, all the donors ran silently past her, soaking wet.

The group shook themselves off and took stock of the situation now that they had escaped the deluge and were back in the Camellia Room.

Holly profusely apologized.

"I am so sorry! I meant to turn off the timers. I even made myself notes! I swear. I am so sorry. You may all use our gym facilities in the Sports Building. We have hairdryers, etc. Again, I am so sorry."

"Well, I'm already dry," said Viola's husband, rubbing his bald head and laughing.

No one in the group would meet her eyes, and she was just about to shepherd them into the Desert Room and outside when she heard Ivy's coolly mocking voice. She was still sitting for her portrait right as Holly and the group had left her twenty minutes before.

"You know, I think the Tropical Forest Room is legit allergic to you by now. You shouldn't be allowed in there anymore. It's just one calamity after another with you, isn't it?" Ivy waited for a beat, and then quietly said under her breath, "Loser!"

Holly took her bait, as she always did.

She spun in her direction and yelled, "Shut up, you privileged jerk!"

The group sucked in a collective breath as Holly took a step toward Ivy. The air crackled with energy, and even Holly didn't know what she would do.

But then, Berkeley came striding into the Camellia Room.

"This is beyond my wildest dreams! You've showered our esteemed donors! Can't you do anything right?" He paused, and Holly stared at her shoes. "Bats, locusts, floods? What's next? The flies and the frogs? You're a walking plague-generator. Get out of my sight! You are on notice: everything better go perfectly at Night Lights, or you'll find your scholarship here at Shellesby College thrown onto the compost heap. Don't mess up again, or you're gone."

Holly's heart was in her throat, and she fled the Camellia Room before she erupted in tears, leaving the donors to gawk after her.

Heather caught up to Holly as she pushed open the door to the Visitor's Center and ran outside.

"Holly, wait. Wait for me."

Holly ran a safe distance away from the greenhouses and waited for Heather on the edge of the Butterfly Garden.

"That wasn't a good look for you. Losing it in front of our biggest donors just gives Berkeley all the ammunition he needs to get rid of you. You know he never forgave you for the locusts eating the Tropical Forest Room. He never will."

"I know he won't! He's just waiting for me to fail!"

"Yes, he is. But you don't need to make it easy for him. Pull yourself together and impress at the Night Lights Ball. Remember, not only your scholarship here is on the line, but also an internship with Ogletree Chocolates. Professor Ogletree is going to announce his decision at the ball. Be the best version of Holly you can be so you have no regrets."

"Thank you." Holly gave her a quick embrace.

"I have to go now, but think about what I said."

After waving a final goodbye, Holly disappeared into the deepest part of the thicket of bushes that comprised the Butterfly Garden. Large butterfly bushes with their deep orange flowers grew tall and meshed with honeysuckle plants, snapdragons, and daisies. They, along with black-eyed Susans, provided butterflies with tasty nectar, as did the huge stalks of sunflowers that loomed over the entire space.

Holly sank deep into these bushes and cried. She knew no one would find her because this part of the Butterfly Garden was left to grow wild, and it was difficult to wade through all of the bushy plants.

Maybe she really was a loser, just like Ivy always said.

Her morale in shreds, she slipped off the high heels she had worn to accompany her pretty dress and lay down on the ground. She was now surrounded by the flowers and hidden from view. Butterflies darted around her and the flowers.

Ignoring the fact that she could get bitten by ticks in this tall, wild, grassy area, she set her phone alarm for half an hour and cried herself to sleep. She'd try to rescue her reputation

KIRA SEAMON

again in a few hours. For now, she felt like she had withered on the vine.

She needed a time out and a reset.

The horoscope she read this morning was right. This was an unlucky day for her.

The world could take care of itself for half an hour.

"Best of luck with that," she muttered before she escaped to sleep.

CHAPTER TWO

"Ow! Stupid cactus!" Holly exclaimed, rubbing her pricked finger. After her time-out in the Butterfly Garden, she'd wound up back here again, working. Currently, she worked on transplanting a cactus that had grown too big for its pot. Unlike William, she always seemed to injure herself when handling the cacti.

William quickly came to investigate. Wordlessly, he took her wrist and led her to the sunniest part of the room. He took his magnifying glass and hovered it over her finger. With a pair of tweezers, he expertly removed the thorn and tossed it into the trash.

He gave her finger a soft kiss and said, "There, good as new."

"Thanks." Holly smiled at him, butterflies in her belly. Every time she looked at him, she was reminded of how attractive he was. He had a razor-sharp haircut that set off his features to perfection. He cut it himself, actually. He had so much experience with pruning he could handle scissors better than any barber. His hair was an amazing chestnut brown with natural blond and red highlights from the sun. He looked like a Greek god to Holly.

"I heard about the flood," he said quietly. "I was ready to run to the woodshop to whip up an ark for you. *Holly's Ark* painted on the side—what do you think?" He gave her a friendly wink.

"Don't 'ark' me, William! I don't think this is funny. Not in the least!"

"Anyone ever tell you you're cute when you're mad?"

"Blistering bluebells! No one in the history of the whole world ever likes being told that!"

"The history of the whole world, huh? And you know that because…"

"Because I am taking World History 101, mister, and at the beginning of chapter seven, it states right off the bat, 'No one in the history of the whole world likes being told they're cute when they're mad!'"

"Holly, you're the best. I can't get enough of you," William said with a laugh. "Come here." He pulled her in for a warm hug and a deep kiss. When they parted, he planted a bonus kiss on her forehead. "Come with me while I weed the lily pond," he urged. "I have to keep working, but you can vent to me while I do."

He led the way through the student nursery and into a magnificent room. They paid this room no mind and continued to the Papyrus Room.

Papyrus plants lined a tiny lily pond that sported a large, stone frog statuette that spurted water out of its mouth when the fountain was turned on. Fat koi lazily swam about, and some lemon-colored gigantic goldfish swished along in there as well.

William sat on the edge of the low stone wall that encircled the lily pond.

"The lily pond's motor has stopped. The fish won't get

enough aeration if I don't get it started again. I think all these lily pad roots have clogged the motor, so I'm going to trim them." He pulled out shears. "Go ahead and rest here and talk all you want."

"Okay, well, just look at this, William! Look at this!" Holly pulled a crumpled soggy piece of newspaper, still wet from the sprinkler deluge, out of her back pocket.

"'Gemini: Today is an exceptionally unlucky day for you,' " she read. "'The only outcome is failure. Stay in bed.' How is that for a depressing *horror*-scope, eh? However, since I am a glass-half-full kind of gal, I disregarded it and came to work today anyway…and see how my decision turned out."

"Are you sure you're a Gemini?" William raised an eyebrow. "I thought with your temper you must be a Scorpio!"

"I'm a Gemini!" Holly insisted.

"Are you sure?"

"Blistering bluebells," Holly swore, "I'm a Gemini!"

"Spoken like a true Scorpio," William said with a wink.

"Will-iam!"

William laughed and chucked an armload of vines to the side. "Well, okay, I guess you're a Gemini. You have your angelic side and your *blistering bluebells* side. Your temper must be due to your red hair."

Holly put a hand up to her temple, pushing her red cloud of curls out of her eyes. "Speaking of that, my hair is all but unmanageable now that it got wet and has air-dried. But I have bigger troubles than that. What have you heard about the flood?"

"Just that all the donors got wet, and Berkeley was so upset he was ready to chew bark."

"It's that Ivy Berkeley! She baited me, and I always react. I can't help myself!"

William surveyed her. She felt like a bug under a microscope being inspected by him. "You're sure this is all her fault?"

"Ivy has been a thorn in my side since high school. You know that. She's so stuck-up and flounces around the campus like she owns the place...which, I guess she kinda does."

"It seems like that," William said sympathetically. "She was definitely born with a silver spoon in her mouth, but you've got to just ignore her."

"Things are worse now than ever! She wants the same internship as I do, and she doesn't even need it. She's so selfish!" Holly took a breath. "And besides that, I overheard her saying the other day that she's also looking forward to me being kicked out so that you would start being interested in her! She's apparently dying to be your girlfriend and totally in love with you. So, now, I'm going to lose both my scholarship and my boyfriend...Just kill me now," Holly muttered morosely.

"Just a minute, little prickly pear! Who said anything about losing your boyfriend? I'm not going anywhere. I love you. I love your drama and your passion and your intensity. I love that you're climbing out of your chrysalis and spreading your wings and shimmering like the gorgeous butterfly you are."

William had stopped weeding now and stood directly in front of her.

"I love your little snub nose, your thin lips, and your high cheekbones. I love your green eyes that spark with energy and anger, and I especially love when they turn the most beautiful sage color when you're excited. Kinda like how they look right now."

"You like my nose, do ya?" Holly asked.

"Absolutely," William breathed, bestowing a kiss on it.

"And you like my lips as well?" Holly asked.

"Absolutely," William answered, bestowing a kiss on them.

"And you like my cheekbones to boot?" Holly giggled.

"Both of them," William answered, planting little butterfly kisses on both cheeks. "Butterfly kisses for my amazing butterfly," he mumbled, busy with his ardor.

"Mmm," Holy murmured. "That's nice." But she suddenly turned away and shifted gears again. "But...but...but...I am not finished processing the flood! I can't bear it. It's so embarrassing."

William said, "Well, you went from high to low; now you need to go from low to *grow*! In the greenhouse, we don't learn from our mistakes. We *grow* from them!"

"I don't *feel* like *growing* right now, okay? I'm so mad I could spit!"

"Why don't you?"

"What?"

"Spit! Go ahead."

"Really?"

"Really. You said it would make you feel better."

"I didn't say it would make me feel better. I just said I am so mad I could spit."

"Then do it."

"Okay." Holly turned her head and spit into the multitude of plants nearby.

"Well?"

"Well, what?"

"Feel better?"

"Not one iota."

William laughed.

"Blistering bluebells, I'm so mad and frustrated and irritated...and...and...and..." Holly started pacing back and forth in agitation.

"That's it! Why don't you give your entire plant-based cuss word vocabulary a good workout? That might make you feel better!" said William.

"Bitter buttercups!"

"Yes!"

"Stinging nettles!"

"Yup!"

"Raging roses!"

"Keep going!" William encouraged her.

"Sizzling sunflowers!"

"You can do better than that!"

"Um…um…hellish hibiscus!"

"Points for creativity!"

"Flaming forsythia!" Holly punctuated this with a couple of energetic fist pumps.

"You are on fire, baby! Keep going!"

"Cursed carnations!"

"Brilliant!"

"Mangled magnolias!"

"*Points* for creativity!"

"Blasted…blasted…um…blasted…"

"Don't stop now!"

"Blasted…um…blasted…um…begonias? Maybe…?"

William laughed. "I think you have wound down now like a top…Are you finished?"

Holly laughed. "Yes."

"Feel better? Are you stable enough for a treat?"

"I'm *always* stable, and yes, I'd like a treat!"

William left the room and quickly returned with a small, sweet beagle puppy in his arms.

"Sweetpea!" Holly shrieked and quickly transferred the puppy to her arms.

The little dog was so excited to see Holly that her tail-wagging became a blur.

The puppy happily squirmed in Holly's arms and licked her arms in earnest. She also made cute little puppy noises.

"I had to bring her with me today because we're here all day decorating, and she's too small to be left alone that long. I set her up nicely in the Science Center lounge, which is now Puppy Central. She has everything she needs."

Holly narrowed her eyes.

"Did you bring her toys?" she questioned sharply.

"You mean the 1,328,476 toys that you bought her? Then, yes."

Holly laughed. She had rescued the puppy around Valentine's Day and given it to William to raise because there was a strict no-dog rule in her dormitory. Holly doted on the puppy, though, and had bought out the local pet stores of all their dog treats and toys.

"Hey, if you're feeling better, we have to get your head back in the game here. We have so much to do!"

"Yes, I'll get started."

"I'll take her for a quick potty walk so she doesn't have an accident in the lounge on Night Lights day."

William left for that, and Holly started tidying the room.

She heard a tiny squeak and looked down to see a miniature red and brown chipmunk at her feet.

A few years back, Boston was in the grip of an extended period of freezing weather, and the night temperatures regularly dipped below -20 degrees. It was on one of these days when William opened the greenhouse to find a half-frozen chipmunk inside next to a hole he had made in a bottom window. He tunneled in for the warmth, and William didn't have the heart to close it up and boot the rodent out.

So, now, he was tame and quite accustomed to the gourmet granola Holly frequently made him.

"Huckleberry! My day is getting better and better by the minute!"

She bent down and scooped the tiny chipmunk up in her hand to inspect him.

"You have the most beautiful fur," she said, admiring his Formula One racing stripe of black and white down his back.

William re-entered right then and said, "Boy, you have had a great ten minutes! Sweetpea and Huckleberry in the same morning! I'll go get him some granola from the kitchen."

When he came back, he poured the delicious nut and grain mixture into Holly's hand, and they both watched how the little chipmunk took some in his small paws and then sat back on his hind legs to munch the goodies. William poured more granola on the floor and straightened up.

"Hey, we'll let Huckleberry enjoy his lunch. Speaking of something, if you are in a better mood now, come with me to the Rainforest Room. I have something to show you. I wanted to wait until you calmed down because it means a lot to me, and I hoped you might be happy for me. Here, come with me."

He led her back to the previous room, which had amazing, rare rainforest plants in it.

"Check this out!"

He tossed her a magazine that said *Horticultural Digest* on the cover. Holly neatly caught it and opened it up to the dog-eared page.

Blaring across the page in huge font was the title: *William Smith, The Rainmaker of Shellesby College's Famous Rainforest Room.* It was a five-page spread with big glossy photos of the Rainforest Room sprinkled throughout the article.

"Five, count 'em, five pages! That's my record. Until now, they've only given me four. Check it out: I'm the *Rainmaker*, baby! Let it rain, let it rainnnn!"

William stomped around in make-believe puddles on the floor. He picked up a garden hose lying along the side of the room and held it upright like an umbrella.

"I'm singing in the rain, just singing in the rain. What a glorious feeling. I'm happy again."

Holly squealed with laughter and applauded.

William jumped up on a large over-turned pot and shifted the hose to now play air guitar while he repeated the verse.

"William, there is no air guitar in that song!"

"There is now, baby!"

Holly exploded again in laughter, clutching her sides.

After a few more seconds of air guitar, William jumped off the pot and lowered his voice considerably.

"Thank you, thank you very much," William said in his Elvis impersonation.

He now held the garden hose like a microphone and said, "My next song is dedicated to my beagle, my very own hound dog, my Sweetpea. Sweetpea, girl, this is for youuuuuuu."

He now launched into Elvis's famous "Hound Dog."

"You ain't nothing but a hound dogggg." With this, he also twirled the hose by holding it tight two feet from the nozzle, then twirling the nozzle in little circles above his head like a lasso.

"Work it, William! Work it!" Holly screamed in laughter.

He did some choice hip swivels as he sang "Hound Dog," sending Holly into peals of laughter.

"William, stop! Stop! Where are you? I can't see I'm crying so hard!"

William dropped his voice even lower and more dramatically.

In his best Elvis voice, he said, "Well, if you can't find *me* darlin', I'll find *you*." He dropped on one knee and gently picked up her hand.

"Thank you, thank you very much," he said in Elvis mode. "My next song, I dedicate to my one and only, to my Holly-Dolly. Little prickly pear, this one's for youuuuuuu."

He now launched into Elvis's famous "I Can't Help Falling in Love with You."

"Take my hand, take my whole life, too, for I can't help

falling in love with you." With that, he gave her hand a soft kiss.

He then jumped up onto an empty potting table and spun around once on his butt, then pushed himself the length of the entire table and slid off the far end.

"Loose, footloose!" William picked up his garden-hose microphone again and kept singing. "Kick off the Sunday shoes..."

He sang the entire song, and then Holly exploded in appreciative applause.

He was breathing heavily and had a million-dollar smile on his face.

"Hoo-wee, that was fun! I am so sweaty now, hoo-boy!"

He splashed some water on his face and then shook his hair.

"William! When are you going to enter that karaoke contest at the coffee shop in town? They're paying $1,000 to the winner of their contest. No one can beat you! That was unbelievable!"

"That was fun." William laughed. "Are you in a better mood now?"

"How can I not be? You are *the* best!"

"Did you read the article?" He went to pick up his magazine. "Look at this. They did a whole spread about our corpse flower plant and our cannonball tree."

Holly and William moved to the front of the corpse flower plant.

"Remember when we got this? Direct from Sumatra in Indonesia? It was so big...twelve- feet-tall! We had to open the roof and crane it in here. It couldn't fit in any of our doors!"

"I remember," Holly said admiringly. "And here you are now, being written up in the magazine for your expert planting of it."

"Here, read the article out loud."

Holly dutifully read, "The Shellesby College greenhouse's Rainforest Room is notable for its cannonball tree. Its malodorous neighbor is the *Titun Arum*, or, as it is more commonly known, the corpse flower, a very rare and unusual plant having a gargantuan solitary blossom spewing out straight upwards from the center of the plant. Its almost nauseating odor becomes overwhelming as the bloom reaches its zenith. Like decaying flesh, the stench can permeate the entire display. Overcompensating for this assault on the olfactory glands is the stunning treat for the eyes—the bloom. Described as the biggest flower in the world, it towers over three meters high above the plant and three meters in circumference and, predictably, draws visitors to it like moths to a flame." She took a breath and glanced up. "I know, William. It is your masterpiece!"

"It is," William said as they stood before the giant flower and admired it. "And to think it will open, which only happens once every decade, right on Night Lights weekend. Can you believe it? Here, read about my cannonball tree miracle!"

Holly continued reading, "William Smith, the master horticulturalist grad student, had grown the behemoth himself from a seed. *Couroupita Guianensis* was a shocker of a tree, with Jurassic-Era-looking flowers developing into cannonball-shaped fruit. The tree was so named not only because of the shape and size of the fruit, but also for the loud report that is made when one of those heavy fruits hits the ground. The fruit has a very strong disagreeable smell in stark contrast to the fragrance of its flowers. Smith has become the first botanist to get the tree to reproduce asexually indoors with his innovative grafting technique." She looked at him in admiration. "William, you are a plant rock star."

"You know what? Damned if I shouldn't ask Berkeley for a letter of recommendation for the Boston Botanical Garden! They are hiring interns now, and I could use that money. I am the legit Rainmaker. I wrote those heartrending letters to our donors to beg them for their donation dollars for the replanting after the locusts. Boy, did they ever open their wallets!"

"I need to thank you for that as well."

"No problem, baby!"

William had also mentioned in the letter to the donors that Berkeley had thrown Holly out as a result of her locust egg disaster, but William asked them to insist that re-admitting Holly to the college was a condition of their donation money.

All the donors readily agreed.

"I can't thank you enough. Without you, I'd be on the compost heap with my scholarship."

"Don't mention it. His punishment was too harsh."

"And Good Golly, Miss Holly Dolly, speaking of an internship with Boston Botanical Garden, if I get one, I am treating you to the most expensive lobster dinner Boston restaurants can provide."

"Mmm, I could use that lobster right now. I'm starving. Drama and tears make me ravenous."

"And I am always starved after my performances. Thank you, thank you very much," he said in his Elvis voice.

"Let's grab lunch!"

"Yes, then we have to buckle down seriously and get this greenhouse ready for Night Lights weekend. We are sooooo behind I'm getting nervous."

"Yes, we'll buckle down and get it done after lunch," Holly agreed.

He looped an arm around her, and they turned toward the exit.

"Elvis has left the building, ladies and gentlemen. Goodnight," said Holly.

William burst out laughing and tickled Holly's ribs.

"You're such a card, baby!"

Holly screamed from the unexpected tickling.

"Stop! Stop, you know I'm ticklish," she howled. William's fingers continued to find purchase in her rib cage. "I'm serious," she rasped, trying to breathe. "Stop! I'm dying. I'm dying. Too late. I'm dead."

"You're so dramatic, Holly-Dolly." William laughed as he stopped tickling her and, instead, kissed her neck.

"I am," she happily agreed. "I can get over anything. I just have to be dramatic first."

William grinned, and with his arm around his girl, they headed off to find lunch.

CHAPTER THREE

*L*ater in the day, Holly frowned at her reflection in the mirror.

"This can't be right!" Holly muttered to herself. She looked like a cross between a panda bear and a raccoon. She had tried to apply a more advanced version of makeup than she was used to, and it was not going well.

"Smokey eye, my foot! I look like I have two *black* eyes." She had not done the proper shading with her eye shadow, and now her large green eyes were encased with a deep black color that spanned her entire eyelid.

"Maybe I should try a different one," Holly mused aloud. She sat in William's bedroom at his dresser. She already had on her pretty crushed velvet black dress and a small heart-shaped diamond pendant. It had been William's birthday gift to her last year. "Let me re-read this article again to see if I can make sense of these instructions."

Holly read her magazine article out loud. "Which Greek Goddess are you? Athena, Venus, or Aphrodite? Check out our makeup tips below to turn heads at your next event! Hmm, that sounds soooooo good, if only I was better at applying makeup."

She had decided to try their Aphrodite look and had been trying to apply the eyeliner to give her a smoky eye effect.

Holly had to wash her face four times already and start over because each time was worse than the last.

"Concentrate, Holly, or you'll be late for the gala. This is your last chance. It's do or die time!" she warned her reflection in the mirror. "So, it says to put the light grey eyeshadow on the inner one-third of my eyelids. Hmm, maybe that's the problem. I don't know where the inner third is."

She got an idea and went to William's desk. Looking around, she found a ruler.

"Ah-ha! Eureka, I got it!" She went back to her position at his dresser and closed her eyes for a quick, small prayer, then held the ruler up to measure her eye. "Ah-ha! Twenty-one millimeters. So, that means the inner one-third of my eye must be from my nose out seven millimeters...right about *here*!" Holly expertly applied the light grey eye shadow to the inner third of her eyelids.

"What a big improvement already! Wow! I'm not a panda bear anymore! Okay, one-third down, two-thirds to go...I can do this!"

Reading further, she said, "Okay, now apply the dark grey eye shadow to the next third of your eye, finishing with the dark brown eye shadow on the outer third of your eyelid."

Holly expertly followed the instructions and sat back in her chair, stunned.

She looked beautiful! She had achieved the desired effect, and now her green eyes were enhanced to perfection.

"Wow, wow, *wow*!" Holly felt encouraged to keep going.

She read the next instructions.

"Now, apply blush to your face with an emphasis on contouring your cheekbones."

"*Contouring* my cheekbones? Who do they think I am, Rembrandt?" Holly said with a groan.

Holly gingerly picked up her blush container as if it were about to bite her. She decided another quick prayer wouldn't go amiss. With a deep breath she muttered, "Okay, I'm going in!"

She glanced nervously at the picture in the magazine and tried her hardest to follow it along her cheekbones. "That turned out pretty good!"

Holly turned her face this way and that, examining it. It may not have been exactly as in the picture, but the blush now accentuated her beautiful high cheekbones.

"Whew! Only the lip left, thank goodness! You got this, Holly!" she encouraged her reflection in the mirror.

"Now apply a thin application of lip liner, making sure to follow the natural curve of your lips. Apply one base coat of lipstick and allow it to dry. Finish shading the outer corners of your lips and apply a second coat of lipstick. Finish with a generous application of a warm-toned lip gloss...What? What? Who knew lips are so complicated! Arggggg!" Holly rifled through her little makeup bag to try to find the necessary items. "Lip liner, lip liner...do I even have that?"

Holly dumped the contents of her makeup bag out on his dresser and realized she hadn't bought one.

"Great! Fine! I wasn't jazzed about that anyway! Yay, I'll skip that and go directly to the lipstick and lip gloss. One less thing to do!"

Finished now with her advanced makeup application, she stared at herself in awe.

She looked like a model and very different from her usually relaxed, natural made-up look.

"Aphrodite is ready for the *world*! Question...is the world ready for *Aphrodite*?" Holly giggled.

"Hey, babe, are you ready to go? We don't want to be late!" William walked into his bedroom.

Holly rose from his dresser and went to stand before him.

"Wow, Holly," William said softly. "You're gorgeous."

"Do you like it?"

"You're the most beautiful woman I've ever seen," William said in heartfelt sincerity.

"Haha, thanks! So…how do you like my smokey eye?"

"Is that what it's called?"

"Yes."

"Well, little prickly pear, as they say, *Where there's smoke, there's fire,* and my heart is ablaze at this very moment."

"Then I got my money's worth!" Holly laughed. "Check it out—here's my article!" Holly showed him the Greek goddess makeup article.

"I see! So, you're Athena, right?"

"No! I'm Aphrodite!" And with that, Holly held the article up to her face to show him the similarities to the Aphrodite instructions.

"No, you're definitely Athena, baby. She was the better one. Smart as well as beautiful. Just like you!"

"But I was going for Aphrodite! You just said yourself I'm the most beautiful woman you have ever seen…ergo…I'm Aphrodite!

"Changed my mind. You're still the most beautiful I've ever seen, but I love your brain as well as your body. You're Athena," William said with finality.

"Hmmph…well, okay…but I didn't do her makeup, and I'm not starting over now!"

"No, you're not starting over. You look perfect, and we're leaving, in fact, right this second! Come on, Athena, I'll escort you to the gala."

William held out his arm, and she curled her arm inside his.

On their way out, he tickled her ribs and whispered in her ear, "Plus, don't forget, Athena has that cool owl."

Holly giggled.

"Oh, yes, you're right! The *owl*! Okay, I'll be Athena for the evening!"

"Thought you'd see it my way, babe," William said with a warm smile as he led her toward the greenhouses.

"Let's do one circuit inside, just to make sure everything is perfect."

They entered the greenhouse, and Holly gasped with pleasure.

"Wow! I haven't seen it since I left here earlier this afternoon, but this is amazing!"

They walked from room to room, and Holly marveled at their handiwork. Both had worked all day to transform the greenhouse into a magical dreamscape.

LED lights were strung along the length of the entire structure of the greenhouses in all the different rooms.

Holly pointed above her head. "Those Japanese painted lanterns look so beautiful!"

"Well, they should. They're Berkeley's heirlooms. His great-great-grandfather was among the first to trade in Japan in the 1800s."

"Of course, he was." Holly sighed. Accolades for the Berkeley family seemed to never stop around here. But truthfully, the lanterns were exquisite. They were joined by twinkly white lights that led upward in a starfish pattern to a hanging cactus piñata. The highlight of the Night Lights Ball would be when the guests hit the piñata and Professor Ogletree's truffles came tumbling down.

"Berkeley told me he just picked up Professor Dudley from the hotel. He said he's going over notes with Professor Dudley and that Professor Ogletree is taking a stroll around campus before dinner."

"And they are the featured guests tonight?" Holly asked.

"Indeed. Dudley is second fiddle to Ogletree, but he runs a rubber empire of his own. Ogletree is so famous in botanical circles, and he's been featured in *Horticultural Digest* so much that they might as well call it *Ogletree Digest* at this point!"

Holly giggled.

"In fact, *Hort Digest* is writing up their presentations tonight. I expect we can read about it in the October edition… hmm…I wonder if we should string up a few more lights?"

"If we string any more lights up, we'll be visible to the space station!" Holly kidded him. "Hey, do you like my wreaths?" Earlier, she had gone downstairs, below the greenhouses, into the herb cellar to bring up some fragrant lavender wreaths she had made from the lavender growing in the herb garden.

"The wreaths are meant to match with the lavender tea I'm serving at the gala afterward."

"They look great, and I can't wait to sample your tea and hors d'oeuvres tonight."

"Tell me the timeline again, William."

"Okay, well, we'll walk to the Science Center and first have dinner in the lobby, catered by the Dainty Pomegranate restaurant. After that, we're going to see a two-hour presentation in the Science Center's auditorium. This will feature the best of the best in the field of botany and horticulture. After that, we'll walk over here for the gala event. The greenhouses don't have as big a capacity as the auditorium has, so only the crème de la crème of guests will attend the gala here in the greenhouse."

"Do you think the Morning Glory Donors will attend the gala?"

"Definitely! Big wigs in the administration, other important alumnae, and of course, that is when Professor Ogletree will announce the winner of his internship award."

"That's the one I applied for! But *Ivy* also applied for it, and she doesn't even need it! She's so selfish. She's probably going to get it because of her family's connections. I'm so upset because I worked my butt off on the application and not only wrote the one paper that it requested, but I wrote two additional papers on the native flora of the Amazon! It took me four months to complete all my research. I virtually lived in the library day and night."

"I know, baby, and I want that internship for you so badly I can taste it. You deserve it. I saw the bibliography you attached. You read the entire Amazon section in the library! I'm impressed...You're almost up to my standard of scholarship," William said with a wink.

"Hey, buddy, I *am* up to your standard in scholarship... You're just a few years older than me...Give me time!"

"Of course, you are! I was just kidding. Like I said earlier, *Athena*, I am as madly in love with your brain as I am with your body," William said and pulled her in for a kiss.

"Hey! Careful, I'm embalmed in two layers of lipstick *and* generous lip gloss. You don't want to mess it up, believe me."

"I see the light!" William laughed and gave her a very brief kiss to keep her lipstick intact.

William's cell phone rang.

"Dang, it's Berkeley. What could he want?"

Holly knew that Director Berkeley thought of William as a son and sometimes asked him to fill in for him when he was unavailable.

William took Berkeley's call. "Yes, sir, no problem. I'll see you in an hour. Goodbye, sir."

"What did he want?"

"Well, Winston, the director of the ornithology department, is out on paternity leave. His wife is due any minute, and so he can't come by tonight and feed the birds."

"Birds? An ornithology department? I didn't know Shellesby had all that!"

"I'm not surprised. Ornithology 101 is so popular it fills up within five minutes of registration in the fall...Speaking of that...you love animals...Would you like to work with the birds?"

"Yes!" Holly's eyes shone at the thought.

"I'll let Winston know, and he'll save a place for you next semester. But right now, I have to go to the roof of the Science Center and feed the birds for the night since he is unavailable. Come with me!"

They turned and walked through the Desert Room.

"Woooo-boy! Look at that! I think she's going to bloom tonight! What a miracle of scheduling."

William retrieved a cloth tape measure from a table nearby and measured a few of the huge blossoms hanging on the night-blooming cereus plant.

"Yup! Four inches in circumference! My fertilizing worked! It's gonna happen, baby!"

"I'm so excited! They're magnificent!"

"Yes, indeed. I am going to invite Professors Ogletree and Dudley back over here at midnight tonight to watch the bloom. I am a little star struck that I'll be able to show off our cereus to these plant rock gods...and it gets even better! Come!"

William gently took her hand and led the way to the Rain-forest Room, and they stood in front of the corpse flower.

"Not only will the cereus bloom, but this old girl is going to open too!" They both marveled at the enormous three-foot-high and three-foot-wide bloom that sat poised to open, like a huge rocket on the launch pad at NASA's Cape Canaveral launch site.

"She is even pickier than the cereus, which blooms only one night a year. She blooms only once every *decade*! To have these botanical stars align, so to speak, with the double bloom is like a miracle!"

They looked in rapt fascination for another minute at the enormous plant.

"Let me lock up and let's boogie to the Science Center so I can feed the birds before the presentation starts."

William led the way out, and they walked over to the Science Center. Holly started to hum "Feed the Birds" from *Mary Poppins*.

William laughed. "If it weren't for that intricate lipstick you have on, I'd go in for another kiss right now!"

"Don't you dare! It took forever to get this on!" Holly laughed ruefully.

"I realize, so I won't…but consider yourself kissed."

Holly immediately started humming "Consider Yourself" from the *Oliver Twist* film.

"Holly, you comic genius! Stop, or I'm turning around and taking you back to the Cot' and the hell with this whole damn gala. You're just too darn cute and funny, and I'd rather spend the night with you than these crusty big wigs, anyway!

Holly laughed, pleased with herself.

"You may be older than me, but I've got your number!" she said and proceeded to fake dial a cell phone.

"Holly/Athena! Stop! Smokey eye, my foot! You are on *fire* tonight, baby! I hope that idiot Ogletree gives you that internship—he couldn't do better than you!"

"Thanks for the vote of confidence," she said, and she leaned into his arm as they entered the elevator.

They got out on the roof and were just in time to see the last of the sunset.

Holly looked around in wonderment. She was now five stories up and could see the layout of the college to the north and the overview of the lake to the south. She felt a small chill up here, as there was a light breeze blowing.

William stood in front of some large bird habitat cages and poured water into the owl and falcon habitats. She marveled at their beauty.

"Wow, I can't believe this! This is the best-kept secret at Shellesby. How did I never find out about the birds?"

"As I said, it's the most popular course here and fills up within minutes of registration. After it's filled, they take it off the roster. So, you probably never even saw it."

Holly admired the sleek feathers of the falcons, and then went to look at the owl section. She saw a snowy owl, a great horned owl, a barn owl, a northern saw-whet owl, and a little guy on the end.

Unlike the others, this one didn't have a name plaque in front of it. It was exceptionally tiny with piercing yellow eyes, a short round body, and almost no neck. She instantly fell in love with it.

"William! There! There's my owl!" Holly was enchanted and couldn't stop admiring the little fluff ball.

"Where? Which one?" William moved to the left and away from the falcon section and followed her finger to see which one she pointed at.

"What's it called? I don't see the name plaque."

William suddenly chuckled, which blossomed into a full-fledged laughing bout.

"What? What's so funny?" Holly narrowed her eyes, suspecting that he was about to make a joke at her expense.

"Well, *Athena,* that *is* your owl. It's called a screech owl, and since you have been known to screech *yourself* a time or two, it couldn't be more appropriate, hot damn!" William finished this with a slap to his thigh; he was so tickled by the coincidence.

Holly had to admit it was funny and joined him in the laughter.

"Okay, I seemed to have walked right into that one."

They continued to the pigeon flock on the other side of the roof.

"What is this?"

"Well, these pigeons have been here since forever. I think the founder of the college may have even started the flock. Each new generation is born and instantly sort of gets absorbed into the system. They're carrier pigeons."

"Oh, like in WWI?"

"Exactly. They're bred to become homing pigeons and can find their way back from distant locales. Here, take a look at Snapdragon."

William gently took out a large, multicolored pigeon and held him in his hands.

"Snapdragon is the leader of the flock, so to speak. He has such great homing instincts I'm sure we could release him in Australia, and he'd find his way home to Shellesby!"

"Really? Wow!" Holly admired the beautiful bird.

"Okay, we're finished!" William put Snapdragon back in the coop. "Everyone is fed and watered. Well, the birds of prey eat live mice, but Winston can dole those out when he comes back after the birth. Yuck, I'm not feeding them their dinner."

"Yuck!" Holly agreed.

"Speaking of dinner, Ms. *Athena*, we have a dinner reservation in the lobby below. Shall I escort you there?" William held out his arm, and she tucked hers inside his. "*Screech* owl, she chooses...priceless." William gave another peal of laughter.

Holly joined him in the laughter, and they were about to head to the elevator when loud male voices stopped them in their tracks. Holly gripped William's forearm as he lead her back to the railing of the roof and they looked down in the direction of the hullabaloo. It was getting very dark, so they couldn't make out who was down there.

"I have been researching you, and I am going to spill all the beans tonight!" Someone threatened below in the bushes right next to the Science Center's back door.

"Don't threaten me, if you know what's good for you," hissed the immediate reply.

"You've been fooling everybody, but you don't fool me, you jerk!"

"I told you once to let it go. If you make me tell you it again, you will bitterly regret it!"

Holly turned to William with her eyes as wide as saucers.

"William, I forgot to give you this article. Here, read this!" She rummaged in her handbag and pulled out the crumpled newspaper article about the dead body in the Providence greenhouse.

William took out his cell phone and illuminated it with the light to read.

"Wow! I hadn't read this," William mumbled as he scanned the article.

Suddenly, they heard a lot of rustling and a muffled scream and other distress sounds.

"I told you to let it go. Here's what happens when you don't!" The mean voice hissed again.

"Come on, let's go down the fire escape stairs and see what's going on."

Holly had misgivings but trailed after William as he illuminated the staircase with his cell phone light.

"Hello? Is anybody there? Do you need help?" William offered to the bushes in the darkness below.

They continued to hear intense rustling and muffled sounds of fighting as they descended to the third floor and peered down into the void of blackness.

"*Argggg!*" someone gurgled in pain.

"It serves you right. I told you to stop sticking your nose where it doesn't belong!"

William turned to Holly and whispered in her ear.

"Holly, I can't believe it, but it sounds like Professor Ogletree!"

"What? How can you know?"

"Well, I watch all his pruning tutorials on Youtube, and I swear, I think that was Professor Ogletree's voice," William said disbelievingly. He leaned over the fire escape railing again and yelled down, "Hello, do you need help?"

There was dead silence for long minutes.

"Ohhh," Holly gasped and pointed out to William a shadowy figure hurrying away from the bushes and heading towards the lake. She squinted hard and thought she even made out a second shadowy figure over on the right. "What was that all about?"

"I don't know. I can't be certain it was Professor Ogletree, though it sure sounded like him. I don't know what went on in those bushes, but we are very late now to the dinner, and Berkeley will be upset if we don't show up soon. I'll text my friend Bill, one of the groundskeepers here, and ask him to check it out. Let's climb back up now and go to the elevator. Here, baby, lean into me. You look cold in that thin dress... gorgeous, but cold."

Grateful for his concern, Holly leaned into him as they climbed back up to the roof so they could take the elevator to the lobby.

When the elevator reached the bottom floor, the door opened, and Holly couldn't believe her eyes. The entire lobby had been turned into a dining area.

It was clearly a black-tie event, with everyone wearing their best formal wear.

Whew, I'm glad I washed off all that black eye shadow I did at first. After all, it's a black-tie, not a black eye, event, Holly thought with a laugh.

More of Berkeley's heirloom lanterns hung on the walls,

and the tables were bedecked with crisp, white tablecloths and candelabras.

"Candelabras!" Holly whispered to William.

"Come, baby, let's find our seats."

They walked up to a person who looked like a manager, as he wore the Shellesby insignia on his suit jacket.

"William! Welcome! Is this your date for the evening? What's her name? I'll check the guest list."

"Her name is Athena," William deadpanned and allowed the manager to browse his list for a minute with his brow furrowing harder every second.

"Athena? I am so sorry, William. I don't see that name."

William laughed. "Sometimes, she goes by the name of Holly Jackson as well. Try that one."

"Ah, here she is. Very good, sir. Please follow me."

Holly elbowed him in the ribs, and they could barely keep from laughing as an usher escorted them to their seats.

"You're at the captain's table, so to speak. The Berkeleys are here, as well as the big donors and some from the administration."

When Holly heard the name Berkeley, her heart sank. *Just my luck,* she fumed, *can I never get my time in the sun without Ivy stealing all the limelight?*

As she sat down, she noticed she was seated directly opposite Ivy.

Ivy was already enjoying the soup, and Holly looked at her with chagrin.

She looked breathtakingly beautiful in a dark blue dress with large diamond drop earrings. As she looked up to her father to tell him how much she enjoyed her soup, Holly caught sight of her face.

She had on the most flawless makeup, far more advanced than Holly's attempt earlier.

Next to Ivy, Holly felt like a grubby orphan who hadn't seen a washcloth in years.

"She even has on *lip liner*," Holly said under her breath in a mixture of admiration and bitterness.

"Holly, Holly. Earth to Holly. Holly, the server wants to know your drink order, baby. Please tell him."

She realized the server must have asked her a question, and she was so lost in thought about Ivy that she hadn't heard.

"Iced tea, please. Light ice, thank you."

"Yes, ma'am."

Holly waited until the server left and then whispered into William's ear.

"I feel so ugly. She's so beautiful. This is the worst thing that could happen. Being seated opposite her, and so now you'll be admiring her perfection all dinner long. Just kill me now," Holly finished with a sigh.

"Where's Ivy?"

"She's right across from me, silly!"

"Where? I don't see her?"

"She's over..." Holly broke off and looked into William's eyes.

His eyes told her everything she needed to know. They were warm and loving, and she knew he was trying to let her know that he only had eyes for her.

"I don't care about Ivy. Not one microscopic millimeter. It's you I love. So, please try to enjoy yourself and forget about her. It's a big night here, and I have a lot to do with the donors later. Please don't make me distracted and worried about you and your jealousy of her. I am yours, and that's the end of it."

She gave him a loving smile of thanks and decided to eliminate Ivy from her thoughts. She turned to her left and was delighted to find Heather sitting next to her.

"Heather, you look amazing!"

She had on a pretty light brown pantsuit with an enormous amber pendant on her necklace.

Holly looked closer and realized there was a dragonfly in the amber.

"Where did you get that? It's exquisite! May I see?" Holly gently held it and looked at the pendant.

"It's my favorite piece of jewelry. I got it in Madagascar when I was there sourcing plants for the National Botanical Garden's collection. It's practically priceless because the dragonfly is completely intact."

"I love it!" Holly admired the pendant until the server came back with her drink.

"Look at all this amazing food! I'll have to write down these dishes so I can try to get the chef in our garden restaurant to recreate this spread."

The theme for the evening meal was a buffet entitled "Around the World in Many Ways" and featured Thai, Indian, and Asian foods that showcased the flavorful fresh produce delivered that morning to The *Dainty Pomegranate* restaurant by Shellesby students.

Holly filled her plate at the buffet and returned to her seat.

"Do you like the yams?" Holly asked Heather.

The purple dwarf yams were given a Filipino flair and paired with a perfectly cooked morsel of tuna with a shredded coconut topping. Indian curries exploded with flavor, utilizing the fresh bay leaves and garlic that had still been growing literally that morning in Shellesby's vegetable garden before the students harvested it and delivered it to *The Dainty Pomegranate*.

"I must get this recipe from the chef, or I will just *die!*" Heather exclaimed as she closed her eyes and spooned in another mouthful to savor.

Thai food dominated the right side of the lobby, and there was a special table in the middle serving an epicurean fantasy of German sauerkraut, red cabbage, and spaetzle with dill cream sauce.

"I see you got a little of the red cabbage. You were lucky! I went up earlier to get some, and there was such a long line. It looked like a twenty-minute wait to get near it." Heather shook her head at that fact.

Holly savored a bite and could understand how the tender red cabbage with the red wine reduction and caraway seeds could make it a crowd favorite.

"Did you get some of the desserts yet? I'm waiting a bit while my body shakes off this food coma I'm in at the moment."

Holly laughed at Heather's admission.

She had surveyed the desserts and found a final two tables were groaning with a cornucopia of desserts, and in keeping with the exotic theme, the purple yams made a reappearance in another Filipino-inspired dish. The yams were mashed and simmered in coconut milk with vanilla beans. The college's fresh vanilla beans were also added to milk and churned to make ice cream as a delightful palate cleanser.

"I happen to love this carrot cake," Holly told Heather, who still sat with her eyes closed in blissful digestion.

The carrot cake was a sturdier dessert choice for those who still had room, and it seemed to Holly that everyone enjoyed munching on the fresh ginger snap cookies.

William turned to her.

"Whew, how are you doing, baby? I ate so much I shocked myself. Their food is so good it should be outlawed."

"I had the best meal in years. Did you hear back from the groundskeeper yet?"

"No, not yet. I'll send him another text."

Holly nodded absentmindedly. She was going to run the Night Lights Ball in a couple of hours and hoped she wouldn't mess anything up this time. Everything had to go off without a hitch. It just had to.

She picked up the last ginger snap cookie on her plate and savored the intense flavor.

This will certainly be a night to remember, Holly thought as she finished her cookie and girded herself for whatever was to come.

CHAPTER FOUR

illiam turned to her. "We should go. The presentation is starting soon, and we want to get a good seat. Let's sit in the back in case I need to slip out to handle anything." He took her hand, and they walked into the auditorium itself.

At the entrance, they stopped to admire a huge gingerbread house.

"Wow," Holly said, "I'm speechless."

They both stared at the huge gingerbread house in the shape of Shellesby College's famous Benefactors' Hall. Benefactors' Hall was one of the oldest buildings on campus and featured the quaint addition of a working carillon in its huge belfry, which was located in the part of the building called The Tower.

"That pastry chef is a genius! I've never seen anything so intricate!" William shook his head in amazement.

He led Holly past the gingerbread house and turned to find seats in the back row. The auditorium was completely filled with important donors and administration workers in the first half of the space, with students filling in the rest of the seats.

As they sat down, he explained, "Well, as you know, Shellesby College's stated mission statement is to *'exceed expectations in education,'* and this gala night features the very best in horticulture, not only here at home, but from abroad as well. From what I heard from Berkeley, this is the most important night on the school's calendar! It's where they get to show off the high standards that make Shellesby the premier institute of higher learning that it is."

Holly nodded in agreement.

"Not to mention, this is the most important night for donations for the college. Seeking to impress the hell out of the big wigs with the big pocketbooks, they're also trying to rake in the donations later tonight at the Nights Lights Ball."

"Well, that food alone would have me emptying my pockets for the school!" Holly patted her stomach and grimaced. "My dress is too tight now, I'm afraid."

William laughed. "Yes, indeed, they say that the path to the heart is via the stomach, and they really scored a home run with that food tonight…oh, shhhhh, it's starting!"

Director Berkeley strode to the podium. "Thank you, everyone. I hope you have enjoyed the delectable food we presented today. We at the college are very proud of our classes' efforts, and we think *The Dainty Pomegranate* outdid themselves and produced a masterpiece today. And, speaking of masterpieces, did anyone see that awesome gingerbread house in the lobby?"

Thunderous applause and wolf-whistles rained down, the audience stamping their approval.

Berkeley continued with the presentation. "Okay, first up is a presentation by Shellesby College Horticultural Club members. They are in charge of cultivating the Sustainable Vegetable Garden, and they provided *The Dainty*

Pomegranate restaurant in West Shireston with the produce that became your dinner this evening. Please welcome to the stage Jared Johnson of the Hort Club."

The audience applauded, and Jared went to the podium. "Thank you very much, Director Berkeley. I am thrilled to share with you some of our jaw-dropping numbers from this year. Favorable weather conditions, along with some horticultural magic from our master horticulturalist grad student, William Smith, made our vegetable crop the biggest in Shellesby history!"

Thunderous applause greeted his words. Holly turned to look at William, who looked a little surprised Jared mentioned him by name.

He bent down to whisper in her ear, "I'm telling you, Holly, with my spread in *Horticultural Digest* and now this acknowledgment, I can almost taste that letter of recommendation from Berkeley and the new job at Boston Botanical Garden!"

Holly laughed. "I hope you get it...and if you do, I can almost taste that lobster dinner."

"Haha, all in good time, little prickly pear. Right now, I can't think of food, but I am pleased as punch for his shout-out, hooo-boy!" William had his million-dollar smile on.

"Soooooo happy for you, but I know you're a plant rock star!"

He gave her hand a gentle squeeze and a kiss. "Shhh, baby, there's more. Let's listen."

Jared went on to discuss how much produce they grew this year and which varieties of lettuces, tomatoes, and beans they'd decided to grow.

"I am extremely pleased to now present a time-lapse film of the growing cycle of one of our big boy tomatoes. We partnered with the film and media department for this. We think it turned out so well we hope to do multiple time-lapse videos of other vegetables next season. So, let's roll the film!"

The auditorium grew dimmer as the film projected onto a screen behind the podium. The audience marveled over the stunning short film that captured the growing cycle of one of these huge tomatoes from the tiny flower, through the green stage, and finally as the giant orb grew enormous and rosy red. The whole thing lasted only a minute but was so popular and the cheering so deafening that Jared directed from the stage that the manager should replay the film.

After the second screening, William turned to Holly. "Wow, that was unbelievable. Tomorrow, I'm going to introduce myself to the film and media department. I want to get in on those films. They look so fun."

Berkeley strode back on stage and shook Jared's hand. Jared exited, and Berkeley further addressed the audience. "Well, I don't know how we can top that, but Keifer Jamison will certainly try his best. Keifer, please come to the podium."

The audience welcomed him onstage, and he shook Berkeley's hand on his way to the podium. "Thank you, Director Berkeley. Well, that big boy tomato is a hard act to follow, but I may just have something here to impress you with."

He now pointed to the back of the auditorium, and the manager dimmed the lights again.

A slide show showed some of the past autumn's Shellesby Farm Fair's vegetable winners with jaw-dropping photos displayed of the prize-winning heirloom tomatoes, giant squashes, and giant pumpkins.

"As you know, the Shellesby Farm Fair is a much-anticipated event in the entire Northeast, and we had a record number of entries this year." He went on to explain that many farmers try to grow these giant Halloween behemoths with the addition of platters of milk.

"Here's how they do it." Keifer gestured behind him as he went through the slides one by one. "As you see here, the farmer cuts the vine of the pumpkin and places the cut part in a platter of milk that is set on the ground. The milk is thought to boost the growth rate of these monsters, which are grown from special seeds, and the milk is thought to maximize their growth potential."

Keifer now paused dramatically.

Holly looked at William with her eyebrows raised, but William only shrugged.

"I have no idea, either, what he's about to say," William whispered to her. They both turned their attention back to the stage.

Keifer continued dramatically, his voice purposefully slowing the pace of his story. "So, since I knew this technique could yield giant pumpkins, I wondered about replacing the regular milk with Muscle Milk. You know the one. It's that creamy dietary supplement that weightlifters use to gain muscle mass. It's brimming with branched-chain amino acids and soy protein."

Keifer paused again for effect. The entire auditorium held its breath, riveted by him. He dramatically changed slides, and the most monstrous pumpkin appeared on the screen. "So, you can imagine how flabbergasted I was when my giant pumpkin topped the scales and weighed in at 2,500lbs! It also won the blue ribbon this year!"

The audience went wild with applause, and the room was abuzz with chatter as people exclaimed to each other about the genius of his idea.

He now proudly showed off photos of his prized produce, and someone in the audience shouted out a suggestion, recommending that he time-lapse film his process next year.

"What a wonderful idea. I think I will!" Keifer beamed with pride. "I'd also just like to add that I donated my pumpkin to *The Dainty Pomegranate,* and they were able to make a hundred pumpkin pies from it, which were donated to the food bank in town."

Cheers and wild applause greeted his last statement.

Berkeley came back onstage and put an arm around his shoulder. Shaking his hand again, he led him off with a smile. "Well, I hardly know what to say next. First, the big boy tomato. Now, the giant pumpkin. But if there's anyone who can top all of that and leave those in the shade...er, the *nightshade*, that is...it's Professors Ogletree and Dudley! Please let me introduce our esteemed guests for the evening. Ladies and gentlemen, Professors Emeritus Ogletree and Dudley."

The audience broke out into the wildest applause of the night. Both professors strode onstage, resplendent in their crisp suits and sharp haircuts.

As Berkeley arranged them onto the seats brought onstage, Holly turned to William. "You have to try to grow one of those monster pumpkins! You can do it. You're the best!"

"Absolutely, little prickly pear! The wheels are turning as we speak." William pointed at his temple.

"Please do one for me for Halloween. I'd love it!"

"Of course, I'll do it for you. We will call it '*Hoctober*' because didn't we agree you're a Scorpio? I'll do it as your birthday present because your birthday must be some-time in October."

"I'm a Gemini!" Holly said with characteristic fero-ciousness.

"Ahhh, you're too easy to tease sometimes," William said with a warm smile and another squeeze of her hand. "What are you going to do with your monster pumpkin?"

"Tsk. Turn it into a carriage, silly! I thought you knew that!" Holly joked.

William laughed. "Well, if my Cinderella commands me to grow a giant pumpkin, then grow one, I shall!" William vowed with a wink. "Oh, Cindy, they're starting again."

Berkeley started his interview.

"We'll start with you, Professor. Can you tell us about your amazing career in horticulture?"

Professor Ogletree cleared his throat and began. "First, I'd like to thank you, Director Berkeley, and Shellesby College for inviting me here again today. I remember my tenure here with great fondness and have always loved my return visits to speak, to teach, and to interact with the faculty and students. Shellesby's students are incredible, and the faculty and facilities are top-notch. It's a pleasure to attend here this evening and share my story."

Berkeley nodded and said, "The pleasure is ours, Professor. Thank you for coming tonight."

Professor Ogletree now turned fully toward the audience and took a deep breath. "Well, I'd like to begin with some personal recollections about my life, which I have never shared publicly before, and then Shellesby College has honored me with an amazing retrospective short film that we will watch afterward. But I'll begin at the beginning, so to speak. Let me take you back to when I was a young sapling."

The audience murmured with laughter at his botanical pun.

"I was so fortunate to receive the Explorer's Grant from the National Museum of Science, along with my esteemed colleague, Professor Dudley. We were lab partners and budding horticulturalists...pardon the pun." Professor Ogletree smiled in response to the smattering of laughter from the crowd. "What a heady time that was." He shook his head in remembrance.

"We were newly minted horticulturalists and botanists, clutching our degrees from the American University of Horticulture and Botany, based then in Alameda in upstate New York, and we were beyond excited to get an internship together at the National Museum of Science. Moving down to NYC was a thrill, and we spent all our free time analyzing the soil composition of Central Park, which we found to include a far larger than expected amount of phosphorus. Ahem...resident city dogs, I'm looking at you!"

The audience laughed again, and he was warming to his subject now.

"Ah, yes...I always had a head for figures, I like to think, and I enjoyed crunching the numbers to figure out optimum water needs and soil composition for specific plants. My colleague, Professor Dudley, was more hands-on, always creating miniature bonsais for our lab office, and he enjoyed pruning, cutting, and shaping the branches of trees. He was always experimenting, trying to discover how a species could be changed into a hardier or higher-yielding version of itself. We were the perfect team, and when our combined research led us to vastly reduce the water consumption at the National Museum of Science's sustainable vegetable garden, we beat out all the other interns on staff there and were rewarded with an all-expense-paid trip to the Amazon jungle in Brazil to try to discover new plants that may be used for medicines or other inventions. We also received an Explorer's Grant, which we shared, and that was to be our seed money for any discoveries we might find."

William turned to Holly, and he whispered in her ear. "You can see why this guy is always in *Horticultural Digest*! Check out that guy over there!" He pointed at a man sitting on the opposite side of the auditorium, also in the back row. "That's Oliver Bilkens, editor of *Horticultural Digest*. He's writing up Ogletree's lecture as we speak."

Holly followed his gaze and noticed a man writing intently in a notebook.

"Wow, we're in the presence of horticultural royalty tonight."

"You bet we are!"

Professor Ogletree had taken a sip from a water glass on

the table next to his chair and now continued. "At this time, the Amazon still had many thousands of square miles totally as yet unexplored—virgin jungles that beckoned to us and turned our whole world upside down. We were to explore a bit further west from the city of Manaus. If you recall, that is the famous city with a world-class opera house in the middle of the steaming jungle. It took us weeks to get to our destination, and we enjoyed the sterling company of our native guides. One guide, in particular, was especially warm towards me, and I shared my dreams of discovery with him and told him of all my research work that I had done in the labs back home.

"His name was Fabio, and his family had helped build the opera house, dating generations back to the opening of the opera house in 1896. His family has been the guides to all manner of explorers and discoverers since then. After a few weeks there, I bemoaned that I hadn't yet found anything notable. Fabio then told me he had heard a legend of a very unusual cacao plant species that grew on Ilha Pequeno."

Holly turned to William in amazement.

William shrugged. "I've never heard about this before! How fascinating!"

Holly nodded in agreement and returned her attention to the stage.

"Now, this was a small island off the coast of Rio de Janeiro, next to Ilha Grande, which at the time was rumored to be run by pirates. I pressed him to elaborate further, but he said he knew almost nothing more except that it was considered to be a miracle cacao species, growing in the sandbars around the island. It's important to note I had studied the cacao tree intimately before I left for the Amazon, and I knew that cacao trees love moisture-rich soil and they grow optimally in the shade. This unusual species of cacao growing in sand bars could indicate a variety that needs less water, so I was instantly intrigued. I inquired how I might get about journeying over there and if it was even safe. We were friends by this point, so I trusted his judgment. He even confided in me and told me about the plight of his fourth daughter, Pomona, who was born with a cleft palate. She was living away from the family, in a hospital in Rio de Janeiro, and on a waiting list for the much-needed operation. The government-sponsored health system there only could afford a few such procedures a year for indigent patients. He told me she had been on the waiting list so long already, and her condition was rapidly worsening. His story touched my heart, so I offered to pay for her surgery myself."

The audience came alive with more murmuring, as they couldn't help but react to this unexpected declaration.

"Fabio broke down and wept and forever more referred to me as his daughter's savior. The Amazon jungle had worked its special magic on me already, and I knew I was forever changed and couldn't possibly downsize my excitement into the little square box of my lab office back in the National Museum of Science. I tendered my resignation from the museum via letter, which they received a good month later, as we were in such a remote locale at the time. I said my good-byes to Professor Dudley, and I felt the spirit of the famed conquistadors stir in me as we traveled for weeks to Rio de Janeiro, where I donated my entire portion of the Explorer's Grant funds I had received."

Holly noticed that at the mention of Professor Dudley's name, Dudley had an angry expression cross his face briefly before he schooled his features back to impassivity as he waited for Professor Ogletree to continue.

Holly nudged William. "Did you see that expression cross Dudley's face?"

"Boy, did I ever. I can't believe it. I thought the two professors were best friends forever. I wonder what's up. Something hidden there, I'm guessing."

They both turned their attention back to Ogletree.

"So, I visited his little girl in the hospital, and the operation, while not a total success, was done nevertheless in the nick of time before her quality of life disintegrated completely. Seeing the relief on her father's face was worth every dollar I donated as he cradled her in his arms. While she was recuperating in the hospital, and before he journeyed back with her to rejoin his family in Manaus, he arranged to get me to Ilha Pequeno.

"Nearby Ilha Grande had been a home consecutively to pirates, lepers, and finally, prisoners, having housed a leper colony for decades, then a top-security prison. All this meant was that the nearby Ilha Pequeno had been largely untouched by mankind. Most explorers deemed it too dangerous because of its proximity to nearby Ilha Grande. However, workers helping in the leper colony and the prison system would notice these strange cacao trees growing in the sandbars that ringed the small island as they gazed at the island while sailing boats to and from Rio. They knew it was a highly unusual variety, but they didn't know what it might signify. So, as soon as he could, Fabio used his connections in Rio to secure me a boat trip out to Ilha Pequeno to examine this unusual cacao variety."

William shook his head at that. "Wow, to be the one to find something that rare! Boy, I wish it could be me someday. I dream about finding rare stuff like that." William looked back at the stage with rapt attention.

"When I was disembarking the boat, I was stunned at the sight of these wild cacao plants growing in the sandbars like mangrove trees! Ilha Pequeno had been cut off from mainland Brazil, and as such, it seemed this variety of cacao tree had adapted to the environment of Ilha Pequeno, and much like the Galapagos Islands, this species developed independently from regular cacao trees. I dug a small tree up and took it back onto the boat. Meanwhile, I had applied, and was successful in earning, a position at the Universidad Botanicale de Rio as a researcher. I subsequently took it back to my lab there and studied it under the microscope. I analyzed its cell structure and found it had adapted to living in the sand by conserving its water needs. I experimented further and took a small snip of a branch and grafted it onto a regular cacao plant. While I could never manage to make the new plant grow in the sand as well, the original plant, with the grafted-on branch, *did* need substantially less water, just like its donor plant did. I eventually calculated it needed 75% less water than regular cacao plants. I was immensely stunned at this discovery!"

William's hand tightened his grip on Holly's unconsciously. "Wooooo boy, I can't believe his luck. Wow, what a find. That guy must be born under a lucky star!"

Holly was absolutely enthralled with Ogletree's story herself. Glancing back at the stage, they heard Ogletree continue.

"I set about trying to buy Ilha Pequeno to assure myself a supply of these highly adapted and specialized trees. Natural selection had allowed the species to evolve undisturbed over centuries on this isolated island off the coast of South America. I took out a loan to buy the island from the government, promising them a 25% cut in profits if I was successful in developing this special cacao tree and boosting the cacao industry. Alas, I never could get the recipient trees to replicate themselves, and unfortunately, the benefits of the water-reduction need evaporated unless a new free graft was placed on it. I grew my Ogletree's chocolate empire out of selling grafts from my cacao trees on Ilha Pequeno to the other cacao growers in the region. The cacao farmers I help around the world with my special grafts see a substantial reduction in their water usage, allowing them to grow cacao trees in many other environments past their native habitat in the Amazon jungle. My grafts have been used on recipient plants in almost arid climates, vastly expanding the number of cacao farms and giving a livelihood to so many."

William whispered to her, "Look at that guy from *Hort Digest*. He can hardly keep up!"

They both glanced over at the editor who was madly flipping the pages of his legal pad, trying to find any additional space to continue to write.

"Ogletree is going to be the entire October edition of *Hort Digest*, I can just see. They won't have space for another word about anyone else." William laughed.

"I can also sell my chocolates cheaper to the public, as my water reduction is greatly helping the factories' bottom lines. The profits I made helped fund my chocolate factories on the mainland in Rio, and I donated a portion of my profits to help fund cleft palate operations around the world for indigent patients. We are now investigating and developing a medicine to help with AIDS research. In conclusion, I would like to offer my most heartfelt gratitude to Fabio, without whom all this wouldn't be possible. Thank you so much, Shellesby College and Director Berkeley, for hosting me today, and thank you, my esteemed audience."

The audience rose to its feet in appreciation.

Professor Ogletree took bow after bow, but the applause continued unabated.

After ten minutes, Berkeley strode back onto the stage and went to the podium. "Thank you all so much for this most generous recognition of Professor Ogletree! He is a marvel in the field of horticulture, and we are so pleased he was able to join us tonight. Here is a short film showing you all those details he just described for you. Please dim the lights."

The auditorium grew dark again, and the audience saw grainy black and white footage of the boat ride over to Ilha Pequeno and archival footage of Professor Ogletree back in his lab at the Universidad Bontanicale de Rio, peering into his microscopic, examining the cacao tree's unusual properties.

The film then segued into the groundbreaking ceremony of Professor Ogletree's first chocolate factory and also showed him doing a graft onto a recipient cacao plant. More footage took viewers on a tour of his chocolate factory, from the beginning of the process to the neatly wrapped Ogletree Chocolate truffles in their square, plastic-wrapped boxes. The audience watched as he visited hospitals and hugged children who had received operations from his foundation, and the last part of the film showed scientists in white lab coats examining the cacao plants for possible medicinal uses.

The film ended, and Professor Ogletree stood again for an ovation from the audience. Smiling, he shook Director Berkeley's hand as he walked off stage, and Berkeley took his spot at the podium to introduce his next speaker.

"I would now like to introduce our next esteemed guest, Professor Dudley, and his rubber plant discovery. Please join me in welcoming Professor Dudley to the stage."

Strong applause accompanied Professor Dudley as he said, "Thank you, thank you. Yes, it sure does bring me back to those heady days in the jungle with my colleague Professor Ogletree! I had lost touch with you, Professor, when you left for Rio de Janeiro, only reading about your discovery in trade magazines and such. What a fascinating journey you have had! Like you, I, too, was bitten by the Amazon bug. I couldn't imagine returning to my little cubicle in NYC either.

"My life took a different turn, though. I continued exploring further west of Manaus, and I eventually was deep in uncharted territory. I realized I could create a map of this deserted jungle, and I became a cartographer for a few years. I was studying methods to reduce insecticides on rubber trees, as arsenic trioxide had been the only effective deterrent to insects. Concerned about the effect of all this arsenic potentially seeping into the groundwater and even into the Amazon River itself, I pondered extensively for years on how to reduce arsenic usage for the trees."

William nudged Holly. "Wow, I can't believe we're hearing all these great stories from these esteemed professors. It's like my early birthday present!"

Holly knew William's birthday was in a few weeks.

"I'm so happy for you, William. I guess that means *I* don't have to get you a present."

"Hey, wait a minute! I didn't say that. I always treasure your presents to me."

"Oh, okay...Your present is still on then," Holly said with a reassuring smile.

William smiled back, and then they continued listening to Dudley.

"Late into my first decade living there, I happened upon a tree one day with a little swarm of insects flying around it. I noticed it was completely devoid of insects on its branches and sought to discover the cause of this boon. It appeared to be secreting a sticky substance that proved to be an effective natural insecticide as well as having anti-bacterial and anti-fungal properties. I was able to grow these special trees from their seeds, and I've grown and shipped the insect-resistant rubber trees worldwide. I have revolutionized the rubber industry by reducing this harmful insecticide, and hopefully, in time, we will be eliminating the use of arsenic in rubber tree farming!"

His remarks were greeted with thunderous applause, and he nodded in recognition at the audience. "I'm afraid I don't have a lovely retrospective film of my life to show you as Professor Ogletree had, but the complete history of my discovery is available to view on my website. Thank you, also, to the very venerable Director Berkeley and everyone at Shellesby College for inviting me here tonight." And with that, Professor Dudley turned and exited the stage right.

Just as Berkeley strode back on stage, William suddenly leaned in to whisper urgently to her. "Holly! You won't believe this!"

Holly turned to look at him with alarm because of the emotion in his voice.

"Bill, the groundskeeper, just texted me back. He said he checked out the back of the Science Building and discovered a dead body in the bushes!"

"A dead body!" Holly forgot herself and spoke much too loudly. She instantly squirmed in embarrassment when seemingly the entire auditorium turned around to look at her and shush her. She even saw Professor Berkeley glance over at her from the stage.

William laughed nervously and immediately swooped in to do damage control.

"Hahaha, this new zombie meme going around on Facebook is so funny! I'm sorry, I just couldn't help sharing it with Holly," William said, thinking quickly on his feet.

Someone from three rows in front of them suddenly joined in and said, "Oh, my goodness, I *saw* that zombie meme. It really is hilarious! I shared it, and it got four hundred likes on my page!"

Another person chimed in from seven seats over and exclaimed, "Is that the one where the zombie is…"

William cut in masterfully right then, "Yes! Yes, that is the exact one!"

The person laughed and continued, "Oh, that one is so funny. I even sent it to my grandmother, and she loved it!"

Berkeley said with an edge to his voice, "Excuse me, excuse me, if I may have your attention again, I'd like to close the proceedings." He glared at William and Holly in the last row, and both tried to sink into their seats and disappear. "Well, my esteemed guests, the presentations are over for this year. But the night is still young, and we have more celebrating to do. If you have a ticket to our Night Lights Ball, please exit and turn down the garden path. It will be held next door in the greenhouses. Thank you, everyone, for coming, and please remember to consider a generous donation to Shellesby College in the lobby on your way out. We have staff waiting to assist you at the table next to the elevators. Thank you again and goodnight-*shade*."

The audience laughed once more, and a tremendous buzz started in the venue. Everyone was aflutter about all they had seen, and they streamed into the lobby.

William grabbed her hand and led her out of the auditorium, and he headed to where Berkeley stood chatting with Professors Ogletree and Dudley.

"William, come over here," Berkeley said this now without an edge in his voice, seemingly over the little hullabaloo minutes ago.

William led her over to the small group of men.

"Professor Ogletree, you know him already, but Professor Dudley, this is William, a master horticulturalist and double doctorate candidate. William, son, I am so proud of all the work you have been doing here. You go above and beyond every single day. I am honored to write you a letter of recommendation for Boston Botanical Garden, and they couldn't possibly get a better intern than you. Congratulations!"

William had on his million-dollar smile and heartily shook Berkeley's hand.

"Thank you, thank you, I am so honored, sir! It's a privilege to study at one of the world's best greenhouse complexes, sir, one I treasure every day, and I could use the money from an internship at Boston Botanical!"

Berkeley beamed with pride at him. "Oh, and this is Holly Jackson. She is a scholarship student here and works in the greenhouse."

It stunned Holly when she heard Berkeley say that in a normal voice with no trace of contempt. He seemed pleased that she had bothered to make herself so presentable for the occasion and could introduce her to his esteemed guests without worry.

I am sooooo glad I did my makeup so well. Whew, thank goodness. I wish I could have gotten that lip liner on, but at least I look presentable enough without it, Holly thought, feeling pleased with herself.

"William, back me up on this…Is it true that our prize night-blooming cereus will open tonight?"

"Seems that way, sir! I just measured the buds right before dinner, and they are at the maximum circumference, indicating a bloom is imminent!"

"Excellent, excellent. Then, I'd like to offer you the wonderful opportunity to have a private viewing of our night-blooming cereus tonight after the Night Lights Ball Gala is finished. I expect the gala will last 'til about 10:00 p.m., and then Holly will be cleaning up for a while afterward."

Both professors looked delighted at the prospect.

"Only thing is, the Desert Room where the cereus is housed isn't very large at all. It's just a special viewing for the two of you, as it has only a capacity for a very limited number of people. Please don't let the 'cereus' out of the bag. We wouldn't want to have to disappoint people and turn them away."

"Night-blooming cereus is one of my favorite plants. I'll be there. I can't wait!" Ogletree exclaimed. "My lips are sealed!" He made a zipping motion with his fingers by his mouth.

"Thank you. I am also happy to accept the invitation. They are indeed a favorite of mine too," Dudley said.

"Wonderful! Wonderful," Berkeley said. "I'll ask you to wait in the Tropical Forest Room on the bench there. Holly will have finished cleaning up by then, and we can do a 'bloom watch' and await the magnificent opening...Usually, it happens around midnight or so. Let's start going over to the greenhouses, then."

Berkeley turned to head the group outside when they were confronted suddenly with loud chanting.

As Professor Ogletree first emerged from the lobby and started across the grassy area to the greenhouses, he was suddenly ambushed by protestors who seemed to appear out of the bushes. A flash mob of student protestors chanted and held large homemade signs up that read: *Workers, not profits!* They chanted: "Hey, Hey—Ho, Ho! Ogletree Chocolates have got to go! Hey! Hey!—Ho! Ho! Ogletree Chocolates have got to go!"

"Holly, quick, let's get back inside!" William grabbed her hand and pulled her back inside the lobby.

"What's going on?"

"Well, I heard a rumor, but I didn't think it was true. I heard that the students who were assigned to create that film retrospective Googled him. They dug up some archived material that they found in investigative reports from Portuguese-language newspapers from Rio de Janerio. These reports examined the working conditions at his chocolate factories. He paid them below minimum wage and did not provide medical benefits for them, despite his oft-mentioned donations to needy children with cleft palates."

Holly was stunned. "I thought he was the most revered horticulturalist on the planet!"

"Well, from the gossip I heard yesterday, workers were interviewed, and they reported that there was even a suspicion of him hiring underage youth. The factories weren't up to code, and they were sweltering there in the humid hot

Brazilian weather. Our American press has been absorbed in the upcoming presidential election, so it didn't pay any attention to foreign-language news reports of irregularities of a certain Professor Ogletree. As such, Professor Ogletree was able to keep his shiny image and burnished it frequently with lecture tours at prestigious colleges all around the world, just like he is here for us tonight."

"Wow, that blows my mind! I guess people aren't all that they seem. He sounds like a real jerk, if this is true!"

"Well, Holly, it seems these are the same protestors who marched last year in Boston. Ogletree's tactics seem to have rubbed them raw, and they seem determined to bring the professor down."

"Hey! Hey!—Ho! Ho! Ogletree Chocolates have got to go! Hey! Hey!—Ho! Ho! Ogletree Chocolates have got to go... workers before profits...boycott Ogletree Chocolates!"

William and Holly stared out at the scene from inside the lobby.

Professor Ogletree looked scandalized, and Berkeley rushed around, calling for campus security. The guards quickly pulled into the parking lot in their SUVs and rounded up the protestors, pushing them back to a corner of the parking lot outside the Science Center building. They kept shouting and yelling, but they were now penned in and herded to a safe distance away from the newly beleaguered professor. Berkeley huddled with Professor Ogletree and spirited him to safety along the path that led to the greenhouses.

"I don't trust them, baby. I have to stay here awhile to close up the auditorium. I don't like the idea of you walking down that path where they can see you. Come with me."

William led her away from the lobby and down a long corridor to a back exit of the Science Center. "Here, this is a lot safer. You are totally out of their line of vision. I don't want you harassed when I'm not around to help you."

"Thank you."

"Look, everything feels a little out of control right now. I am shaken up about the dead body behind the building, but this is the most important night of both of our careers. I am about to meet both those professors and show off my botany skills when the night-blooming cereus opens up later. After all, without my fertilizing technique, they'd still be in buds for another three nights. And *you* literally need to get that internship with Ogletree. He's announcing his decision in a few minutes. Remember, people are presumed innocent until proven guilty, and I have no proof whatsoever that Ogletree was involved with that incident behind the building earlier. It was too dark for me see anything."

"You are right, William. My mind is all awhirl with everything going on, and I agree with you about the internship. Let's just see if I even get it, and then we can decide if Ogletree is a shady character or not."

"Baby, you look so gorgeous he'd be blind not to choose you. You deserve it."

"I am so happy for you! You got your letter of recommendation! You are the plant rock star, as I always say!"

"You'd better start calling Boston seafood restaurants and make reservations at them all. Lobster dinners every night this week!"

"I can't wait." Holly laughed.

"Bill told me he isn't even going to break the news to Berkeley just yet. He said he has secured the area and wants to wait until the Night Lights Ball goes off without a hitch. We will talk to Bill and discuss everything the minute the gala is finished. Right now, we need to concentrate on the biggest night of our careers. Go out that door in the back and hustle over to the greenhouses. I'll be there as soon as I can. Bye, Athena."

"Love you, William."

William turned to go, and she continued down the long corridor leading to the back door. As she moved, she heard a voice.

"Yes, what a jerk! I was about ready to strangle him right there on stage!"

Holly gasped as she recognized the rasp of Professor Dudley.

Another corridor branched off from the one she was in, and she gingerly turned left to follow his voice. He paced back and forth in a darkened classroom as he vented to someone on his cell phone.

Holly hid in an adjoining darkened empty classroom, her ear pressed to the wall.

"Yes, yes, the protestors are out there right now, even as we speak! I guess I'm not the only one who isn't enamored with the *esteemed* professor!"

Holly's eyes widened.

"And that blasted 'retrospective'! Give me a break! They whitewashed all the large sections of his life, particularly those sections about me!"

Holly felt a prickle of apprehension as she realized she was in a remote part of the mostly empty Science Center and wondered if she should leave.

"First off, the dear professor neglected to mention that the Explorer's Grant was only partially funded by the time we left for Rio. The remainder of the grant was to be paid to us both, upon our return from Brazil. When Ogletree tendered his letter of resignation and disappeared to Rio, the Museum took it very poorly and considered it a dereliction of duty. As his colleague, they lumped *me* into Ogletree's misdeeds and decided to terminate *me* and withhold the remainder of the Explorer's Grant."

At this point, Holly knew she couldn't leave without hearing the rest of this shocking story.

"So, since Ogletree had made off with the first down payment from the grant, I lost my position with the museum, and they fired me! Do you know how hard I had to scramble to find any employment down there? That's how I became a cartographer, which, while interesting, failed to provide me with an adequate income."

Holly listened, spellbound.

"I became *persona non grata* in the museum world, as the museum made it known that they held both him and me in disrepute and cautioned other museums against hiring me. Can you believe it? I was so experienced and passionate about botany, and now I was suddenly with no job prospects and no information about Ogletree's whereabouts. I was abandoned and betrayed by him!" Dudley wailed to his listener on the phone.

Holly held her breath, transfixed by all this new information.

"And the fact that he never *once* tried to contact me and abandoned me in the jungle, well, I don't have to tell you that festering sore spot has now morphed into a vendetta at this point. I'm going to confront him tonight and tell him how I feel!"

Holly decided she had heard enough, and Dudley seemed to be finishing up his call.

She scooted down the hall as fast as her high heels would allow her to and turned back onto the other corridor. She headed for the exit with her mind awhirl.

Holly had just heard a bombshell admission from Dudley and wondered what shape his explosion would take. Pushing through the door, she hustled in the darkness toward the greenhouses. She had to set up there before all the guests arrived, and now she was late. Walking as fast as her heels would allow, she headed to the Night Lights Ball Gala and her destiny. Ogletree was going to announce his new intern soon, and she prayed it was her.

She felt conflicted about him at this point—what with the protestors, the incident they witnessed from the roof, and all she learned about the gossip surrounding Ogletree from William. Dudley just seemed to confirm a possible real dark underbelly to the esteemed Professor Ogletree, but beggars can't be choosers. She needed the internship, and badly! Still shook up from always skating on thin ice with Director Berkeley, she decided to turn a blind eye to Ogletree's possible seediness and would consider herself fortunate if she ended up as his apprentice and all that would mean for her financial security.

"It's showtime," Holly said to herself and walked to the door of the greenhouses. "Do or die."

Opening the door, she gave a quick prayer and hoped for the best.

CHAPTER FIVE

"*H*olly, I'm going to gain ten pounds just tonight alone! This food is so scrumptious. You are a fantastic chef, young lady!"

Holly set out a light buffet for the guests in the Camellia Room. The assemblage waited in the Tropical Forest, Rainforest, and Papyrus Rooms, and any minute now, the Night Lights Ball Gala would begin.

Heather joined her in setting out the displays of food.

Holly's theme was *A Summer's Bounty*.

She had spent days preparing all this food, and now the Camellia Room was stuffed with huge, folding tables featuring heaping platters of food which guests could sample with small plates and cutlery laid out for them.

"Mmmmmm…young lady, just what is in this dish? You are a culinary magician!" Heather held a plate and sampled the dishes one by one.

"Well, that is fresh steamed cauliflower sprinkled with aged parmesan mixed with baby broccoli florets with a sharp cheddar sauce."

"Divine. And your beet salad is yummy," Heather said as

she scooped heirloom yellow and red beets with huge slabs of fresh tomatoes in a red wine vinaigrette onto her plate. "Is this it? It certainly lives up to your billing, my girl!"

"Yup, it's my world-famous ratatouille. Pretty tasty, if I do say so myself!" Holly indulged herself and spooned some of her warm veggie mixture onto a plate as well. Her show-stopping ratatouille featured onions, tomatoes, carrots, and just about every other root vegetable from the college's gardens. "How about my bean salad?" she asked, fishing for compliments.

"Mmmmmm," was Heather's mumbled response, as her mouth was too full to speak.

Holly looked down at her creation. The wild colorings of the different featured heirloom bean varieties created a kaleidoscope of color, as she had sliced, flash-cooked, and then tossed them with a silky balsamic vinaigrette.

"Which variety of onions, Holly?" Heather asked, helping herself to tantalizing onion tartlets along with points of toasted bruschetta, which itself featured the big boy tomatoes shown earlier in the time-lapse film.

"Those are actually shallots and Vidalia onions."

"Perfection," Heather announced.

Small paper cups were filled with fresh leek and potato soup, which was kept warm in large, heated tureens next to the onion tartlets. Moving farther along the tables, there were different lettuces and salads. Boston lettuce was cloaked in a fresh bleu cheese dressing with chunks of pancetta and small cherry tomatoes.

"Caesar, my favorite! I amend my earlier statement. I am gaining twenty pounds right this *second!*"

Holly laughed. Her classic Caesar salad showcased the college's romaine lettuce varieties, and there was a tender salad featuring a soft mixture of the delicious, blushed oak leaf and burgundy butterhead lettuces. This was drizzled with a light dill dressing, and generous handfuls of hazelnuts brought out the natural nutty flavor of these greens.

"Waldorf!" Heather ascended to the highest realms of food ecstasy as she eagerly spooned a scoop of Holly's creation. She had given the classic Waldorf salad an unusual twist with the substitution of shredded Chinese cabbage instead of the usual bed of greens.

Holly finished off the display of food with her root vegetable salad. Heirloom carrots that were startlingly purple and yellow in color were dressed in a unique honey-lemon remoulade, with the honey she collected that morning from the college's apiary.

"You must become a chef. You are so ultra-talented. I can't stand it. If you don't open your own restaurant, please come down to National Botanical Gardens and teach our chefs your recipes. How about a little getaway during vacation week?"

"Hey, I'd love to visit you down there. Let's plan on that!" Holly gave Heather a quick hug.

Just then, the door burst open, and Berkeley poked his head in.

"I'm sorry, but they can't be kept at bay any longer. The Night Lights Gala is officially open!"

The guests streamed in and gravitated to the buffet area. Holly smiled and played her hostess with the mostest part very well. She went to greet Jasmine and Jessamine along with her new friends, Violet and Viola.

She didn't see William anywhere and figured he was still locking up the science auditorium.

Holly did see Ivy, however, angling next to Ogletree as he was due to announce his decision very shortly. This was Holly's cue to turn back into the Visitor's Center kitchen to prepare her tea selections, a.k.a. her ace-in-the-hole.

Pushing open the screen door that led to the kitchen, Holly

felt her adrenaline surge as she thought about what she was about to do. It was risky, perhaps, but necessary.

She was determined to get the internship and wanted Ivy out of her way for once.

Since she knew Berkeley invited Ogletree and Dudley for the private bloom party at midnight, she would brew something she could serve to Ivy to make sure she didn't accompany her father to the party. Something harmless. Something effective.

"Your time is up, Ivy! You'll have to return to your dorm to sleep and let me have a chance to shine without you hogging all the limelight for once!" Holly muttered under her breath. "I need this. You don't.

"If I can just get Ogletree on my own, I *know* I can convince him to let me be his intern!" Holly continued muttering.

As she dreamt of Ivy's comeuppance, she busily cut open dozens of coconuts, reaming out the coconut meat and making the coconut shell bowls presentable as teacups for the guests.

The college's famed herb garden would be showcased tonight with the guests sipping elegant and unusual herbal teas from the coconut shell bowls she prepared. Mint, oregano, thyme, rosemary, lavender, basil, chervil, cilantro, dill, fennel, lemon grass, parsley, sage, sorrel, and tarragon would all be crushed and blended by her in the most magnificent ways, creating truly original teas sure to stun the guests with her originality and creativity.

She quickly toasted up the coconut meat in the oven and sprinkled it on cookie sheets, creating tempting, bite-sized chunks. Once finished, she would serve them in cucumber shot glasses with Professor Ogletree's chocolate drizzled over them.

Holly made her cucumber shot glasses by cutting and hollowing out cucumbers, creating a vegetable version of shot glasses. The discarded cucumber remains she left marinating in a bowl with her special herb vinaigrette she enjoyed making. She often basted summer vegetables with it, and it was a highlight for the frequent barbecues she held on warm summer nights.

"Mmm, this cucumber salad is for me while I clean up after the ball!" Holly tasted her creation and pronounced it satisfactory, then put a dish of it away to eat later.

She snatched a bit of the toasted coconut meat off the cookie tray right as the delectable sweet treats came out of the oven.

Honestly, her genius tonight was in part credited to her English Lit class. She couldn't take all of the credit.

As part of her English Literature class requirements, she'd had to read Shakespeare's *Romeo and Juliet* and discuss it with her study group. One part that really captured her imagination was when Friar Lawrence gave Juliet a potion to fake her death.

Freshly installed in her new job as a student worker in the greenhouses, Holly was instantly curious about which exact herbs they might be. She scoured the internet, finally Googling "Friar Lawrence herbs," and found an obscure farmer in Louth, Lincolnshire County in England.

"Friar Lawrence herbs...who knew?"

Holly now moved to the stove and very carefully placed a few of these delicate herbs in a bit of cheesecloth and simmered them in a pot on very low heat.

She had stumbled upon his blog when she searched the internet where the farmer wrote he grew them as a palliative cure for his wife, who suffered from end-stage Alzheimer's.

Unable to bear the suffering of his bride, he investigated what herbs might bring about short-term relief from her most painful episodes. Then, he cultivated these herbs and blogged about his experiences and outcomes with them. He wrote that the herbal tea he brewed with them produced an extremely strong calming effect, like a potent sleeping draught, and that the effect lasted for a few hours.

A few harmless hours.

Which is just perfect for tonight. Holly smiled.

"There! It's finished. I simmered them for five minutes, just as he instructed."

Determined to try his unique brew, she'd messaged him and inquired where she might find these herbs. He generously sent her clippings from his garden, and Holly set to work cultivating them in Shellesby's pristine herb garden.

Oh, if those stuffed shirts in administration only knew what else was growing in their perfect herb garden, Holly thought.

"Holly, it's almost showtime! Keep pushing, girl. I think Ogletree is going to announce his decision any minute now!" Holly encouraged herself.

All her industriousness in exotic herb cultivation would be repaid tonight when she could serve up Shellesby's resident "Juliet" some Friar Lawrence herb tea!

The tea wouldn't hurt her. After all, that farmer in Louth loved his wife and would never harm her. However, Holly hoped the powerful blend of the herbs would hopefully put Ivy into a deep sleep, almost a trance-like state—the very state that helped calm the farmer's ill wife during her violent episodes.

Holly dumped a large shot of honey from a jar into the tea and placed that cup very carefully on the table.

"I'll deploy you later," Holly said with a mischievous smile.

She now filled her serving tray with coconut shell cups of the amazing herbal tea blends she had made earlier. She backed out of the door and immediately circulated around the guests and dispensed the fresh hot tea.

"Holly, there you are! Everybody, and I mean everybody,

can't stop talking about your food. Congratulations, young lady, on a runaway success!"

Holly smiled at Heather.

"Wow! What a compliment! Thanks!" Holly handed Heather one of her coconut shells filled with tea.

After seemingly an eternity, Holly felt the time was right to stop serving everyone else and concentrate on Ogletree.

She glided up to Professor Ogletree and offered him his own chocolate poured over the coconut. The Professor smiled at this presentation, accepted a cucumber shot glass, and thoughtfully munched on the contents.

Well, well, well? Holly could hardly bear the wait.

The professor took his time, savoring the treat until he chewed and swallowed the very last coconut piece. He ate so preternaturally slowly that Holly was convinced she could practically see his salivary alpha-amylase enzymes digest the coconut completely, leaving the hydrochloric acid in his stomach with virtually nothing further to digest.

Could he drag the suspense out any further?

He then slowly withdrew a handkerchief from his pocket and wiped his mouth and chocolate-covered hands.

By this time, Holly was almost beside herself with anticipation.

"Amazing, my dear...just amazing. You are clearly very talented. I am impressed with your originality, creativity, and execution of design. Perhaps next year, I might consider you to be my intern."

Sucking in a breath, Holly stared at him. "Next year?"

He gave her a cursory glance. "This year, I am more than happy with the delightful Ivy and am not currently accepting any further applications. But, well done, girl. Chin up, you'll go far!" Professor Ogletree said, dashing poor Holly's hopes of financial freedom to the ground.

Unable to believe that all her efforts had turned up fruitless, Holly's lips tightened into an angry line as she spun on her heel wordlessly and went in the immediate search for "the delightful Ivy."

She literally had to change Professor Ogletree's mind. Her entire future depended on it.

Ivy was currently busily pouring salt in Holly's wound by excitedly telling her friends, knowing Holly was nearby. She looked the picture of happiness, giggling about her latest success. Ivy pranced around as though she'd just won the lottery.

Holly burned with envy and jealousy toward her.

She couldn't bear the thought of the torturous mocking Ivy was sure to visit upon her.

Swept up in her swirling emotions, Holly looked around wildly and spotted something. It was a nice round seed pod that had fallen off the dwarf horse chestnut tree planted nearby.

Perfect! Holly thought.

She scooped it out of the dirt and rolled it like a bowling ball to stop directly in Ivy's path, some eight feet in front of her.

Holly immediately scooted to the far end of the room to put as much distance between herself and Ivy as possible.

It was a perfect crime, Holly thought. *She won't be able to link it to me. After all, I'm all the way down here,* she reasoned.

Ivy was completely oblivious of the pathway as she giggled up a storm with her friends, and her voice got more and more animated as she expounded upon her vast good fortune.

"I swear, I didn't know he'd pick me," she gushed. "Although, I didn't have much competition, did I?" She gazed slyly at Holly, who somehow remained unreactive.

Instead, Holly watched, rapt from the far edge of the room.

Ivy didn't see the seed pod in the pathway. She was too busy trying to stick it to Holly.

Suddenly, Ivy's foot stepped directly on it, and she skated a few inches forward, teetering in her high heels.

"Whoa! What's this?" Ivy screamed.

She looked like she may have turned her ankle a bit as she grasped her friend's arm.

"Ivy, are you okay?" Her friends gathered around.

Ivy stood stock-still and looked down at what caused her to fall. She then kicked the seed pod out of the way and slowly looked around the room.

Eventually, her eyes sought out Holly's at the far end of the room.

"These pathways were supposed to have been *swept*," she said angrily. "I'll have to make sure my father knows that they weren't!"

Holly quickly lowered her gaze and started clearing a table. She peeked up to see what was going on and saw Ivy give her one last stare, then turn and walk away.

Ivy could never prove Holly had done it on purpose, but somehow, Ivy always managed to come up roses. She still had a way to get Holly in trouble! Because, yes, in fact, Holly was supposed to have swept the paths. Which she had done. Before she purposely rolled the pod into Ivy's way.

Holly had turned away to carry a tray back into the Visitor's Center kitchen when she felt a tapping on her shoulder. The tap stopped her in her tracks.

Nooooo, she thought to herself. Does the man have eyes in the back of his head? Wasn't he off in the Papyrus Room, discussing the koi?

Can't she just be left to enjoy a little sweet, sweet revenge on Ivy just this once?

The tapping got more insistent on her shoulder.

With a deep sigh, she turned and faced him.

William's eyes sparked with anger, and he pointed one imperious finger toward the student nursery door.

Yikes, she thought. She was in for it now. William was the most nurturing and loving person she had ever known. He encouraged her endlessly with almost limitless patience for her foibles, but occasionally, she snapped his patience in two. This looked like one of those times.

His mind worked in botanical ways.

A master gardener, he couldn't help but nurture her as well.

For sunshine, he gave her his warmest smiles.

For water, he gave her his best advice.

For fertilizer, he gave her strong encouragement.

She felt so bonded to him she would prefer to lose a limb than to lose him.

They were so close he was bonded to her on almost an instinctual level.

Everything was great, except he also thought his role as mentor to her included occasional "prunings." In fact, he probably thought she needed a little pruning right now. From the look of him, it would be quite a pruning indeed.

She walked to the far side of the room that led to the student nursery and opened the door. She heard him walk in behind her and close the door.

Facing away from him, she waited for his next move.

"Did you?"

"Yes," Holly replied the minute the words left his mouth. She knew he had seen Ivy teeter and was trying to confirm if she was the author of the mishap.

"Face me," William commanded.

Her shoulders drooped, and she took thirty seconds to turn around, but when she did, all her resolve slipped, and she felt the tears start.

"No! Dry up, right now! You look absolutely gorgeous, and you are not going to ruin that with the waterworks. Stop it, right this second."

Holly knew that if he had talked softly to her, she would have indeed dissolved into a puddle, so he was actually trying to be kind. His voice stung, nevertheless.

"You have enough personality for twenty people, and you are an absolutely brilliant young woman. You could have a 4.0 if you applied yourself consistently."

Holly was now locked onto his eyes and gave him her undivided attention.

"The other day, when you were studying at my Cot' and fell asleep, I leaned over and read the paper you are writing for World History. You're doing excellent work. You are a brilliant, gorgeous young woman who can leave Ivy in the dust if you just stop these childish temper tantrums."

"Well, maybe I'm all that, but it wasn't enough to get the internship."

"Baby, I know you are devastated, and I am crushed for you too. You deserve it. Life isn't always fair, but you have to control yourself. Ivy is envious of you! When will you understand that?"

"Well, she has a nice big fat internship to console herself with."

"I know that, but darn it, Holly! Do you really need Berkeley to dress you down in front of everybody again? Think! Stop throwing tantrums like an eight-year-old girl whose teddy bear lost an eye."

"It was a pretty nifty little crime, though, if I do say so myself. Did you see her teetering? That was choice!"

"It will not feel so choice when Berkeley calls you out on it."

Holly listened to him intently. The sounds of the party had receded, and her world narrowed down to only William and her. He *had* decided to do a little pruning with her, and boy, it stung.

William looked at his watch. "Listen, it's eight o'clock.

Bedtime for eight-year-old girls with teddy bear issues. Do you need to go back to your dorm and get to bed, or are you going to march out there and show Ivy what a powerhouse young lady you are?"

"I'm not sleepy, William."

William let out a huge breath. "Okay, prickly pear. Come here. Stop getting in your own way." He pulled her in for a warm embrace, taking care not to give her a kiss lest he ruin the lipstick she still had on. Leading her to the door, he opened it.

"William, there you are! The donors are waiting for you. You promised to tell them how we craned in the corpse flower plant into the Rainforest Room."

"Ahhh, one of my favorite stories. I'll be right there."

He gave Holly a wink and a thumbs up.

"*I believe in you*," he mouthed, and he walked with Berkeley toward the Rainforest Room.

Holly turned on her heel, walked briskly toward the Visitor's Center kitchen, and banged her way in, leaving the door to slam behind her.

She carefully put Ivy's coconut shell cup with the Friar Lawrence tea on the leftmost side of her tray. Then, she filled the tray with more of the regular herb tea in the cups and turned to walk back out to the party.

Maybe she was a powerhouse young woman, but...she would be that tomorrow. Holly laughed silently to herself.

Tonight, she planned to indulge her inner eight-year-old self and see to Ivy's downfall. She had been tormented by Ivy enough, and now, it was payback time.

Maybe she did have some Scorpio in her, after all.

She vowed to get her birth chart done, just to see. Holly had a strong revenge instinct, that was for sure. And revenge is best served cold. Or, in Ivy's case, hot tea.

Making sure the tea was arranged correctly on her tray, she waltzed back out in search of a little more trouble.

With a determined stride, she served her tea sweetly to all the guests until she had only two cups left on her tray. Ivy's spiked tea on the left and one last regular cup of tea. Ivy clung to her father's arm, beguiling him with the joy of her impending internship with Professor Ogletree and chattering away like a magpie.

Zeroing in on her target with narrowed eyes, Holly barely had time to compose herself to a more genial state as she waltzed over to Ivy. She was closing in when she felt restrained by a hand on her arm. Professor Dudley stopped her in her tracks.

"My dear, you couldn't possibly let me leave here without sampling some of your much- praised gems!" Professor Dudley exclaimed.

Holly tried to tap down the howl of frustration she felt like emitting. It was all she could do not to stamp her foot.

Wondering if steam was escaping from her ears, a clearly disappointed Holly slapped on a fake smile and offered Professor Dudley a cucumber shot glass and held out the last remaining coconut shell cup of regular lavender tea. Holly kept a death grip on Ivy's Friar Lawrence herb tea with her left hand.

She felt checkmated as she saw the glimmer of interest and intrigue flood Professor Dudley's over-alert eyes.

"I smell such an unusual aroma from that cup in your left hand. It is piquing my interest to the breaking point! Come, let me take a sip and satisfy my curiosity!" Professor Dudley said.

Holly felt her stomach drop to her knees. She couldn't believe this. This couldn't be happening!

Somehow, Professor Dudley's expert horticulturalist nose had smelled a rat, and now he enjoyed tormenting her, as he sensed she was up to something.

Damn the man, Holly thought. *Could his super sensitive nose actually be correctly identifying those strange herbs she just brewed up?*

Suddenly, Professor Dudley covered his hand over hers, trying to wrest it from her. Her hand tightened on Ivy's coconut shell bowl to the point that the bones of her fingers popped out starkly against her skin, almost skeletally.

Ye Gods, how did this sinkhole of a problem just pop up out of thin air? Holly silently screamed this thought.

Through gritted teeth, she spat out, "This one is for me, Professor. I need something a little stronger than the rest to recover after my hostess duties tonight. If you just release me, I'll go enjoy it back in the Visitor's Center."

His suspicions of smelling a rat confirmed, Professor Dudley looked to take an altogether inappropriate joy in watching Holly scramble to weave her web of lies. He tightened his hand over hers, determined to wrest the bowl out of her grasp.

Holly was feeling panic set in when she suddenly heard a very loud crack, and a startling noise made her jump. The guests took turns using a palm frond to try to bang open a cactus-shaped piñata, the party game to cap off the night. Hung from the Guadalupe palm in the Tropical Forest Room, the piñata spilled down dozens of wrapped Ogletree Chocolate truffles to the floor, spurring spontaneous applause and chuckling.

As the guests dropped to their hands and knees in their expensive swanky clothes, scrambling to find the goodies now hiding amongst the pots of plants and palms, Holly recovered her composure faster than Professor Dudley and, with an authoritative spin on her heel, wrested her hand off his and marched toward her true target, Ivy.

She fearlessly strode toward her arch-nemesis.

Part of her squirmed in embarrassment because she was

the serving girl at this party. Ivy's privilege meant she hadn't worked a day in her life. But a bigger part of her enjoyed Ivy's nascent comeuppance at the hands of the special tea she was holding in a death grip of her left hand.

"Hello, Ivy! I'd like to congratulate you on your upcoming internship. I know you'll do a good job and gain valuable experience. I brewed this special tea just for you, using the honey from our apiary—the sweetest honey for your sweet victory!"

It wasn't exactly a lie because without tasting the Friar Lawrence herb tea she didn't know how unpalatable it might taste, so she overcompensated for any ill flavor by pouring practically a half cup of honey into Ivy's tea to mask the flavor. *So,* there was *honey in the tea...There were just some strong herbs as well,* Holly thought.

The ruse worked. The honey worked. Down her gullet, Ivy poured the entire contents of the coconut shell bowl, even licking her lips afterward, so much did she enjoy that sweet taste.

"Ah, yes, thank you, Holly. How very appropriate that *you* serve me the celebratory tea. I'd say that I'm sorry to have to say goodbye to you, but…well, we both know that I am not."

Holly gave her a look and then left her as Ivy resumed telling her father how happy she was with her new job. Holly started clearing the used dishes the guests had left lying around on the tables. After about eight minutes, she heard Ivy suddenly exclaim how sleepy she suddenly felt.

"My eyes feel like they have lead weights on them! I can't keep them open much longer!" Ivy mentioned loudly to her father. "I guess I didn't sleep well last night from all of the excitement."

Holly's ears perked up as she imagined her sleeping draught must be taking effect.

Berkeley looked a little alarmed at how fast Ivy seemed to be wilting.

"You've got to take better care of yourself, darling," he told her, holding her arm as he ushered her around the Tropical Forest Room, saying her goodbyes to the administrators and the professors.

This was Holly's cue to smartly exit the party. She planned on being far away from the hullabaloo when the tea finally hit Ivy's unsuspecting system in full.

She slipped out of the Camellia Room through the west screen door, abandoned the trays she had been holding all night onto a table, and sped through the unpopulated parts of the greenhouse. Holly quickly pushed through to the utility closet, where she stripped out of her party dress and heels and changed into the jeans, top, and sneakers she would wear later when she cleaned up after the ball.

Holly was just pushing her way through the back door into the Botanical Gardens when she heard Berkeley yell, "Call 911 immediately!"

Holly froze in her tracks.

What? 911? Ivy is just supposed to be sleeping! An ambulance is certainly overkill. Holy Holly-hocks!

She rushed outside to await events. She didn't have to wait long.

CHAPTER SIX

*H*olly decided she'd better stay hidden to be on the safe side. The last thing she needed was for Professor Berkeley to toss her out on the spot.

From the shadows, she saw Ivy turn to her father, white-faced.

"Daddy, I think I'm gonna faint," she said weakly. She then swooned beautifully in his arms, and he half dragged, half carried her through the Camellia and Desert Rooms and carefully laid her down, stretched out on a table in the Visitor's Center.

"Call 911 immediately!" he said frantically, his eyes wildly scanning the crowd.

Rosemary, his secretary, ran to the office phone and dialed the ambulance.

Meanwhile, another hullabaloo began to take shape outside the greenhouses.

When the cactus-shaped piñata spilled its horde of Ogletree Chocolates and the truffles rained down, the protestors outside the greenhouse became inflamed anew and resumed their chants.

Campus security didn't allow them to come inside the Night Lights Ball, but they let them stand outside and watch the proceedings, their noses pressed up against the windows of the Camellia Room. But now, shouts of "Hey, hey! Ho, ho! Ogletree Chocolates have got to go!" resumed with increased vigor as the protestors saw the Glitterati eagerly scoop up the truffles from the floor, oblivious and uncaring of the workers' plight in Ogletree's candy factories.

"Hey, hey! Ho, ho! Ogletree Chocolates have got to go!" screamed the protestors. "Workers over profits!"

"Yikes! This is turning into a bona fide ruckus!" Holly muttered before she ran the twenty feet across the small greenhouse parking lot and disappeared into the darkness of the Botanical Garden.

She saw campus security quickly respond and herd the screaming protestors away from the greenhouses and back to the Science Building. Meanwhile, West Shireston Emergency Services over-responded, as they usually did, and sent three fire trucks and two ambulances to the greenhouses in response to the 911 call for help.

All the emergency vehicles pulled up in dramatic fashion, stampeding up the narrow driveway and into the parking lot in front of the greenhouses. Their sirens blared as they approached, and their rotating red emergency lights provided a type of strobe effect, lighting up the greenhouses like a disco.

"What an unusual addition to the Night Lights Ball!" Holly whispered to herself. "This is a bona fide ruckus, indeed!"

It didn't escape her attention that she stood at the root of the hubbub.

The emergency personnel piled out of their vehicles, and soon firefighters and EMTs streamed into the Visitor Center's door, shoving a gurney along with them. They loaded Ivy onto it and assessed her vital signs.

Then, they pushed the stretcher quickly out the door and

parked it next to the ambulance to continue their assessment of her. She was now sleeping, half-reclined backward on the stretcher, and they covered her with a blanket.

Holly heard the EMTs say that she appeared to be sleeping deeply, none the worse for wear, though they mentioned her heart rate and breathing rate were markedly slow but still normal. Holly sighed deeply in relief.

None the worse for wear.

Whew!

They took a health history from her father and asked if she'd eaten or drank anything unusual.

He thought on that, and then narrowed his eyes.

"She did drink a cup of something that Holly served her," he said slowly. "I don't know if that's related, but come to think of it, she did start complaining of sleepiness a few minutes later."

The EMT scribbled this down, and Holly shrank into the bushes. This wasn't good.

"By the way, where is Holly?" Berkeley yelled to no one in particular.

Oh, man.

Holly watched as the EMTs tried waking Ivy up, but she was quite dead to the world, and they were loathed to try more invasive measures.

"We're taking her to Mt. Cedar Hospital, where she'll remain for observation, sir."

The guests hadn't dispersed at all, though they were all now crowded together in the parking lot, along with the emergency vehicles. They hadn't seen this much excitement in quite a while.

The administrators and donors were visibly shaken by Ivy's fainting, and they wanted to stick around and watch the proceedings.

Suddenly, Ivy struggled to sit upright, even managing to

slide off the stretcher and stand wobbly on her feet. Her eyes were now open but in a weird, unblinking way. It was clear she was still asleep! She suddenly lurched forward and started to sleepwalk around the parking lot.

"To be or not to be! That is the question!" announced a clearly somnambulant Ivy in a booming voice suitable for an outdoor Shakespeare performance. "Whether 'tis nobler in the mind to suffer the slings and arrows of outrageous fortune or to take arms against a sea of troubles and by opposing end them."

Ivy now explored her own outrageous fortune and suddenly became agitated in her sleep-induced trance. She had completely startled and shocked the onlookers and emergency personnel when she hopped off the stretcher and delivered her monologue. They reached out their hands toward her to help guide her back to the stretcher and soothe her, but she rounded on them so fiercely, teeth bared, that they shrank back and thought it best not to increase her agitated state.

Holly clapped a hand over her mouth, lest she yelp with surprise and give away her hiding spot.

"Oh my goodness, oh my goodness...what is happening here?" Holly muttered inaudibly.

"Is this a dagger which I see before me, the handle toward my hand?" Ivy intoned. She had now maneuvered the blanket they had used to cover her shoulders and clasped it with her left hand around her throat, the blanket fluttering out behind her like a makeshift cape in the gentle breeze as she strode about.

She paused and contemplated her outstretched right hand and appeared frightened of the possible invisible dagger she imagined she held there.

"Out damned spot! Out, I say!" She effortlessly segued into the world-famous Lady Macbeth scene, the imaginary dagger in her hand now effortlessly morphing into imaginary blood dripping from her hand.

Still in turmoil, she loudly cackled, "Double, double, toil and trouble, fire burn and cauldron bubble!" She pivoted fiercely on her heel and yanked at the blanket with her left hand.

Holly was spellbound. She hadn't meant for this to happen, but boy, oh boy, oh boy. Ivy's comeuppance was *spectacular*! The carefully crafted, curated image Ivy presented to the world had disappeared, and she knew people would never quite look at "Princess Ivy" the same way again.

"This is *priceless*," Holly breathed.

Turning again suddenly, Ivy muttered, "Nothing will come of nothing" and stalked onward, exclaiming that, "the better part of valor is discretion."

Calming down slowly, Ivy now strode considerably more tranquilly toward the crowd lining the right side of the parking lot by the Butterfly Garden, and they parted for her in a hurry, like the Red Sea parted for Moses. She made her way through the throng gathered there and stopped when she reached one of the rose bushes in the Butterfly Garden.

"What's in a name? A rose by any other name would smell as sweet," Ivy purred and decided then and there to stop and, verily, smell the roses. Straightening up, she continued with a gentle pace, still clasping the blanket around her like an impromptu costume.

"This is very midsummer madness," she murmured. "Uneasy lies the head that wears the crown." And with that, she regally strode toward the greenhouse, all festooned with lights visible from outside, the red emergency vehicles' flashing rotating lights now shining on the greenhouses as a backdrop of theatrical lighting to this impromptu outdoor Shakespearean performance from Ivy.

"But soft, what light from yonder window breaks?" Ivy spoke, mesmerized. Tiptoeing from the Butterfly Garden back to the greenhouses, she gazed in awe at the lighting effects on the airy window-filled structure.

"Shall I compare thee to a summer's day?" she crooned to the greenhouses as she stood in awe outside them. Her moods were rapidly changeable now, like out-of-control windshield wipers. She suddenly fell into a morose, contemplative mood.

Staring into the greenhouses from the outside, she leaned her right hand upon the glass and spoke.

"All that glistens is not gold. There is nothing good or bad, but thinking makes it so."

At this point, Berkeley motioned wildly for the EMTs to "do something," and they tried once again to approach and soothe her, attempting to guide her back to the stretcher.

"Et tu, Brute?" shrieked a wild-eyed Ivy, twirling around on her heel to face them suddenly as they tried gently approaching her from behind. "Get thee to a nunnery!"

All eyes were riveted onto her, and she elicited a couple of titters from the crowd at the absurd appropriateness of her quotes.

The EMTs immediately shrank back again, aghast at this turn of events, while a clearly troubled and entranced Ivy was held mercilessly by her hallucinations.

Holly watched all this from the protective darkness of the Botanical Gardens. She was absolutely agog at this scene before her. That farmer in Louth, England never once mentioned that his Friar Lawrence Herb Tea had possible hallucinogenic side effects. Apparently, this strong tea that had calmed his wife had an opposite, paradoxical effect on Ivy.

After getting over her complete shock at this most stunning and unexpected of developments, Holly now settled back and actually started enjoying the show.

Ivy had performed in every Shakespeare production in high school and at Shellesby and, of course, studied and read most of Shakespeare's famous plays and works in her honors English classes. Hundreds of quotes were stored in her brain, and they all seemed to pour out of her now in her vulnerable state.

A somewhat indifferent performer when awake, she had morphed into a passionate Shakespearean actor now, imbuing her quotes of the famous bard with more energy and life than anyone had ever seen her do before.

Giving her finest performance yet, in short, Ivy seemed to be able to pull out of herself infinitely more depth of true and natural emotion when she was in this sleeping, walking trance than when she was awake and burdened down by society's expectations of the perfect princess her father and everyone else expected her to be.

The true Ivy, it seemed, needed a potent tea to loosen up her inhibitions. *Forget the purported loosening effect on the tongue of wine*, Holly thought. This *gangbuster* tea she had brewed up loosened Ivy's tongue faster than a teenager loosening his tie after his first formal.

As if reading Holly's thoughts, Ivy continued suddenly. "*We know what we are, but know not what we may be,*" Ivy said in a stage whisper as she glided from the greenhouses back to the stretcher area.

Still clasping the blanket closed at her throat like a cloak, she made her way along her path. Her audience, the administrators and donors, along with her father and the medical personnel, all thought she might bring this startling performance to an end.

But then, she suddenly continued.

"Some are born great, some achieve greatness, and some have greatness thrust upon them," Ivy remarked, even in her heavily compromised state, she somehow was enjoying the rapt attention from the audience. Some corner of her brain seemed to have noticed that she had a captive audience, and the latent showgirl in Ivy suddenly showed up, and she simply couldn't get off the stage.

Suddenly refreshed, she launched into a completely admirable attempt of Act II, *Midsummer Night's Dream*. "I know a bank where the wild thyme blows, where oxlips and the nodding violet grows, quite over-canopied with luscious woodbine, with sweet musk-roses and with eglantine: there sleeps Titania sometimes of the night, lulled in these flowers with dances and delight."

Having reached Shellesby's famous Herb Garden, Ivy sank gracefully right in the middle of the herbs and knelt there, whispering, "I must go seek some dewdrops here, and hang a pearl in every cowslip's ear."

Leaning down and breathing in deeply of the pleasant aroma of the bed of basil where she had gracefully dropped herself into, she continued with the oft-quoted *Merchant of Venice* line:

"How sweet the moonlight sleeps upon this bank."

Gazing straight upward now at the moon which shone brightly, having recently emerged from a bank of clouds, she rose gracefully to her feet and began to dance barefoot amongst the herbs, trampling them underfoot.

The EMTs had removed her high heels when they loaded her onto the stretcher, and now Ivy twirled and danced in the dirt of the Herb Garden, shedding her inhibitions as surely as she smashed the tender herbs underfoot. A delicious aroma wafted up from the Herb Garden as her mashing and smashing of the herbs released their fresh scent—an herb version of *pigeage*, a French term for grape stomping. She was transformed into a Bacchanalian Maiden, arms reaching skyward as she twirled careful about, as she continued from *A*

Midsummer Night's Dream.

"Sweet moon, I thank thee for thy sunny beams, I thank thee, moon, for shining now so bright; for by their gracious, golden, glittering gleams, I trust to take of truest this by sight."

Her spontaneous dance finished, Ivy picked her way out of the Herb Garden, fishing her blanket up off the ground, where she had discarded it when she flung her arms in the air while she danced.

Dragging the blanket behind her like a spent slugger dragging her bat back to the dugout after nine long innings, Ivy made her way back to the stretcher area, past the onlookers and her absolutely mortified father. Her recent exertions had fatigued her, and she looked around for a place to rest. She made her way to the stretcher and gingerly sat down on it, swinging her dirty feet up onto it.

She laid her head back and spoke her most effective words, whispered with a shivering emotionally poignant quality.

"We are such stuff as dreams are made on; and our little life is rounded with sleep."

With that, Ivy closed her eyes and sank into a peaceful, albeit deep sleep, the hallucinations finished, and the potent tea's effect wearing off.

It was such a shocking turn of events and so deeply entertaining the onlookers were hard-pressed to not applaud the "performance." There was now a fevered murmuring amongst the administrators and donors as they tried to process and discuss all they just saw.

The EMTs rushed the stretcher into the ambulance and slammed the door closed, utterly relieved that this most unusual patient had finally wound down, like a top, without further incident.

"I'm going with her!" Berkeley declared. Before he got in, he pulled William aside and spoke in his ear for a minute.

William nodded, then Berkeley quickly vaulted inside, and the ambulances left.

Holly gave a bird call from inside the Botanical Garden. She saw William's head snap up and instantly look over at the Botanical Garden, as she knew he would guess it was her. He quickly slipped down the stone staircase to the Botanical Garden where she waited below. Holly emerged from her spot in the overgrowth, and both beheld each other with huge, shocked expressions.

"Your dainty fingerprints are all over this caper. I know it! What did you give that poor girl to drink? By god, it was the most animated I ever saw her...when Ivy was asleep and sleepwalking!" William had to laugh despite himself.

"I never expected that to happen," Holly blurted out. "I gave her a special herb tea that some farmer in the middle of England gives his Alzheimer's wife, to calm her during violent episodes. He never mentioned hallucinations or sleepwalking as a possible side effect."

Holly worried a bit despite her gloating over Ivy's downfall. If her scholarship was already in jeopardy before tonight, this tea caper with Ivy would surely send Director Berkeley over the edge. *I might as well kiss Shellesby College goodbye right now*, she thought grimly.

William laughed. "I am going to save the lecture because, baby, you have done some real humdingers in your life, but you really hit the *jackpot* here. Ivy was hysterical!"

"She had it coming, believe me, but boy did I get a great return on my investment! Those herbs cost me $9.99, but Ivy's comeuppance tonight was priceless!"

"*Hurricane Holly* blew through the Night Lights Ball! My gosh, you're a Cat 5 if I ever saw one!"

"*Hurricane Holly.* I like that. Has a nice ring."

"Ever since I met you, I feel like my life is in the spin cycle in the washing machine. Most days, I don't know up from down anymore, but you take us all on a hell of a ride, I can tell you that."

Holly laughed. "You're welcome. Don't mention it."

"Listen, Berkeley is really going to chew bark over this one, and it'll be all I can do so he doesn't chew a stripe off you! I gotta go now. Berkeley wants me with him at the hospital. I'm taking my car. He wants to get Ivy settled there and then have me continue to keep an eye on Ivy. He might need to come back here eventually to pick up Professor Dudley to bring him back to his hotels. He just told me that he offered him to stay over here in a dorm overnight in case he's busy with Ivy for a long while. Anyway, please tell Professors Ogletree and Dudley that the cereus viewing is off. Lock up the greenhouse and text me when you're done so I know you're safe."

"I mean…it was good, though, wasn't it?"

"I'm speechless. *Vintage* Holly, that's all I can say."

Holly laughed. "Okay, I'll text you."

Stunned by the entire evening and dismayed Ivy had destroyed the herb garden with her twirling, Holly contemplated the huge amount of work it would be tomorrow to replant the herb garden from scratch.

That was, if she wasn't kicked out of Shellesby once Berkeley got back from the hospital.

She went back to her perch in the overgrowth and watched from there as the guests gossiped amongst themselves, discussing both the Night Lights Ball and Ivy's performance.

It started to gently drizzle, which eventually put an end to the gossiping, and the administrators and donors made their way to their expensive cars lining the parking lot.

Holly saw Professor Dudley say his goodbye to Rosemary, and she wondered where Professor Ogletree might be. She hadn't seen him during the entire episode with Ivy. Holly was supposed to catch both professors to tell them the private viewing was off, per William's request.

She watched as Professor Dudley walked Rosemary to her car and was about to emerge from the Botanical Garden when she realized her hands were dirty from holding onto the branches as she hid in the overgrowth. Holly wiped her hands on her pants and was lost in thought when a hand suddenly reached around her, pulled her upright, and stifled her scream.

It was Professor Dudley!

"Shhh! I knew you were hiding here. I could see your silhouette hidden here in the trees. Your eyes were gleaming like a cat's in the moonlight. For such a smart girl, you really should take better pains to cover your tracks," he admonished. With him still covering her mouth, she heard his whiskey-smooth voice purr in her ear as he held her fast against him.

"I know what you put in her tea. How inventive! I could smell the different herbs a mile away when you circulated as hostess of the ball earlier. You cemented my suspicions when you were scared to death to let me take a sip of that tea. I knew then it was not a regular black tea. I had never heard of tea made from lobelia, heliotrope, and pipizintzintli to have hallu-cinatory side effects—at least, I think those are the herbs you brewed for that firecracker brew! How unusual and rare! I never heard of sleepwalking and trances as possible effects either. But there was our girl, Ivy, 'Poisoned Ivy,' performing a Shakespeare Greatest Hits Show in front of our very eyes," Dudley snarked. "Stunning performance, I do say. I didn't know she had it in her...I far prefer Ivy asleep than I do awake."

He paused to laugh. "I salute you, though, girl. I happen to like your spunk. I want to offer you an internship with my company...Take care not to serve me any of your *special* teas, though." Professor Dudley laughed at his joke.

Holly thought a tornado had blown through her brain, her thoughts going 170 mph, scattering in all directions. *What?* Professor Dudley's intern? *What?* Right when she thought she was finished here at Shellesby, here sprouted a completely new and unexpected opportunity. She had no time to contemplate further, though, because suddenly, Professor Dudley spoke again.

"Here, this is something to think about," he said as he pressed a thousand dollars in cash into the back pocket of her pants. "I have to go now and prune some of the dead wood in my life. I want you to do one thing for me tonight, and your internship is secure. Leave the area *immediately*. Don't come back to the greenhouses until morning and don't speak about what we discussed here with anyone. Those are my only terms, and then financial freedom and an internship are yours."

Holly didn't need to be told twice.

She fled the Botanical Gardens and disappeared down the path that led away from the greenhouses. The now-deserted parking lot was clear of people, emergency vehicles, and campus security. As Holly ran, she spared one thought for Professor Ogletree. She saw he had hidden in the Visitor Center's office when the protestors started chanting again after the piñata broke, and he likely missed all the hullabaloo with Ivy outside.

"Oh, well," she muttered. "Dudley told me to leave now. I better do that, and Ogletree can take care of himself."

Realizing that since William hadn't had time to go back and update him as to the cancellation of the private viewing of the night-blooming cereus, he likely wouldn't know the updated schedule. For all she knew, he expected William and Berkeley to appear at any moment as the clock inched its way toward midnight now.

Not my problem anymore, Holly thought as she sped to her dorm.

Savoring Ivy's downfall and the fact that she had come out

on top this time, she climbed the stairs to her room and slammed the door.

"She who laughs last laughs best," she reminded herself. With a deep sigh of satisfaction, she lay down on her bed to rest.

CHAPTER SEVEN

*H*olly's head had no sooner hit her pillow when she heard her phone ring and saw an unfamiliar number display on it. She imagined it might have been Berkeley calling from the hospital.

He must have gotten my number from William, Holly thought.

She ignored the call because she knew he'd be furious with her, and she didn't feel up to that level of stress now that it was already close to midnight.

Immediately after that call ended, she heard her phone ring again and saw William's name on her phone. She would always answer his call, no matter the time.

"Hello?"

"Hi, baby, Ivy is getting put through the wringer here. They're taking samples of everything to try and identify those herbs. I'll be here another hour at least. Did you lock up the greenhouses?"

"Um, well, um, no."

"Baby, you need to! We have a ton of precious plants in there, and Berkeley will kill me if they suddenly walked off, so to speak. You have to secure the plant collections."

Holly was torn between wanting to obey him and the strong admonishment she had just been given from Dudley, who was possibly her new employer.

"Okay, I will, right this second." Holly decided she didn't want to be responsible if some plants were stolen out of the unlocked greenhouse, so she decided she'd better go back and lock up. She'd just be quiet, and Dudley would never know the difference.

"Okay, thanks. Call me, babe, when you're done. I want to know you're safe in bed before I go to sleep tonight."

"I will."

Holly threw her clothes back on and started toward the greenhouses. As she approached, she suddenly saw the lights go off. This was extremely dramatic because only one second earlier the entire place was ablaze with every light burning. The Japanese lanterns were on, the hundreds of LED lights were on, and of course, all the major lights in each room.

And suddenly, the greenhouse was now dark.

Feeling extremely apprehensive, she realized the only explanation was that someone had turned them off...or cut the power.

Someone was in the greenhouses right this very second.

But who?

She noticed the emergency exit door was also open a crack.

Feeling a panic attack come on, she wondered if someone was in the process *right this very second* of stealing some of the precious rare plants William had just mentioned.

Boy, he'd scold her to kingdom come if she'd allowed a theft in there because she hadn't locked up the greenhouses. Feeling nauseous with anxiety, she decided she had no choice but to see what the hell was going on.

Holly slipped through the crack in the emergency door and took stock.

She heard the sprinklers on in the Tropical Forest Room.

What? Sprinklers?

She then heard loud voices and decided to hide herself behind the golden barrel cactus.

It was so monstrous that if she crouched down and folded herself into origami she stayed completely hidden. She held her breath and listened, soon recognizing the cultured voice of Professor Ogletree and the rasp of Professor Dudley.

"Well, well, well," began Professor Dudley. "I want to share with you all the frustration and heartache I've been living with all these years, and watching your film retrospective tonight was like rubbing salt into the wounds!" Dudley stormed.

Holly gasped. Apparently, he was confronting Ogletree now at midnight as they were alone in the greenhouse. Holly was aghast. She couldn't believe she would have missed all this if she had stayed in her dorm room. What was going on with Dudley anyway? Why was he so angry? He sounded like he was reacting on pure emotion. Probably driven by the demons that might have been stirred to life ever since he heard Ogletree's smug lecture, she guessed. She held her breath, crouched down even lower behind the cactus, and listened.

"I have nothing to do with you," Ogletree sneered. "I made my fortune with my innovation and cleverness, and you didn't have anything to do with it."

"I taught you the grafting technique way back in Ackerley College when we first met. It was our team science project that won us that grant to explore the Amazon, and while you were busy doing soil sampling or using the neutron moisture meter, I was busy developing the grafting technique! After you came back from Rio, you lied to me and never told me about your discovery! You claimed to have wanderlust and a sudden inability to return to the confines of the National Museum and wanted to live the bohemian horticulturalist's life in the Amazon Jungle. How did you think I felt when I read in *Horti-*

cultural Digest a year later about your 'amazing' find and grafting technique?"

"You had no part in my discovery," Professor Ogletree retorted. "I gave that man my grant money to pay for his little girl's surgery without asking for anything in return. When he led me to the cacao plant, I recognized the value of it and moved heaven and earth to bring that plantation into existence. You hadn't yet patented that technique, so I broke no laws in using it myself. I just applied it in a most lucrative way —that's all. You should have applied for a patent."

"Patent? Patent?" Professor Dudley screeched apocalyptically. "We were colleagues in college, working on research together for that grant. I didn't know I had to patent a technique that I was using for shared experiments with my co-worker! And it wasn't your grant money alone! Half of it was mine. *Mine!* Do you hear me? How do you think I felt when I was terminated by the museum when they received your letter of resignation? They viewed it as you being derelict in your commitment, and so they canceled the remaining payment of the Explorer's Grant!

"I lost my job and my money because of you. You never contacted me once. You abandoned me there with no afterthought. And if it weren't for me and my initial discovery of those plants growing in the hot sun, your precious Fabio wouldn't have ever thought to disclose to you those plants on Ilha Pequeno. It was *my* find that triggered his disclosure, and then of all things, he discloses it only to you because you gave him money...which was *my* money too, by the way! So, you cost me my job, my reputation, my money, and then sailed off to conquer the world and leave me forgotten! What a nasty, selfish jerk you are!"

As this fiery exchange was all done amid complete darkness, Holly realized the darkness actually provided a cloak of anonymity to the proceedings, encouraging each man to make his deepest utterances, the darkness almost lending a confessional-like quality to the invective. The only light was a bit of moonlight once in awhile as the moon played hide and seek with the cloud cover.

"You always were the lesser scientist compared to me," Professor Ogletree preened arrogantly. "I was the brains behind the grant, anyway. Without me, you would never have found your way to the Amazon and your precious rubber plant empire. You should thank me for delivering you down there."

"If you don't show some compassion, I'll strangle you with a garden hose!" Professor Dudley wailed, incensed. Their angry voices echoed and bounced off the windows of the empty greenhouse. The sounds ricocheted every which way, morphing the glass structure into a type of grotesque carnival fun house.

Holly left the Desert Room where she had been hiding and sneaked into the Camellia Room. She was now only one room away from the action in the Tropical Forest Room. She hid under one of the tables on the side wall and watched the proceedings through one of the bottom windows.

Professor Ogletree suddenly seemed to become aware of the isolated nature of the greenhouses and wondered aloud where William might be. The sprinklers were on, but both men stayed dry, as the sprinklers were angled away from the bench where Professor Ogletree sat.

"He isn't coming tonight. The viewing of the cereus is off. He went with Ivy and her father to the hospital."

This news seemed to greatly alarm Professor Ogletree, who now realized he was set up and cornered by Professor Dudley, who obviously knew the updated schedule.

Sensing he had to get out of the greenhouses in a hurry, Professor Ogletree lunged from the bench. Holly saw Professor Dudley had been circling Professor Ogletree in the darkness and was now only four feet behind him as he sat on the bench.

He suddenly pushed forward a ten-foot potted palm, so it fell alongside the bench, blocking Professor Ogletree's exit onto the circular path. Ogletree's only option was to now hack his way through plants on the other side of the bench, but they were so densely planted they created a thicket of palms and torch ginger with large, exposed roots he knew he'd trip on. Settling back down on the bench and pondering what to do next, he waited for Dudley to make his next chess move.

Holly stood rooted to her spot. She dared not disturb such an emotionally charged scene. Hidden under the table and peering through the bottom window of the room next door to the action, she held her breath to see what came next.

"I want my fair share of the chocolate empire. I want my name on the chocolates too. It was my grafting technique that let you ride to botanical 'super-novadom,' and I want people to know that it was my invention that you exploited. Without the grafting technique, your star cacao plant would be just another freak of nature on a forgotten island in the ocean!"

Hearing his beloved cacao plant described as a freak of nature, Professor Ogletree dug in despite the danger of the surroundings.

"*Go away!* I'll never make you a partner in Ogletree Chocolates! *I am* Ogletree Chocolate, founder and discoverer of the most amazing cacao plant in the world. Enjoy your success as a rubber baron and get a life already!"

"And another thing. Maybe this will change your mind! I finished up doing my notes with Berkeley earlier this evening and went outside for a stroll. I saw you with that student protestor and the shoving match that you instigated. I saw you push him down, and I didn't see him get back up. Did you kill him like you killed the other student the other day down in Providence?"

"Dudley, you have egregiously overstepped the mark. How dare you?"

"How dare I? I've got the goods on you for that murder too. The only reason I have not turned you in is that I am giving you one last chance to give me half of your chocolate empire… the half that is rightly mine!"

"Oh, for goodness sake, you loser, you will *never* be a part of Ogletree Chocolate. Get that in your head already!"

Dudley grabbed some palm fronds and shredded them with anger. It seemed to Holly that he was pushed beyond all reason at hearing such a decisive and derogatory reply. She thought he must have reached the boiling point of frustration of living in Professor Ogletree's shadow. Indeed, the shade probably felt unendurable for Dudley at this point, having up until now been unaware of his former colleague's arrogance and poor opinion of him. Now, having heard his superior attitude, Professor Dudley's anger suddenly started to froth.

Leaving the bench area, she saw him feel his way into the Rainforest Room.

Holly couldn't see the Rainforest Room from her angle, so she waited with bated breath to see what would happen next. Dudley instantly reemerged into the Tropical Forest Room. He had apparently gotten out his pocketknife and sawed off one of the cannonballs from the cannonball tree and stowed it under his arm like a football.

Flinging off rubber gloves he had "borrowed" from the greenhouse's utility room in disgust, he apparently wanted nothing to interfere with his aim.

Professor Ogletree heard these movements and tried to feel his way past the downed palm tree to the right of the bench. He seemed to Dudley a shadowy figure lurking to his left side, across from the bench on the circular pathway. Professor Ogletree looked like he was calculating his escape route when suddenly a cannonball fruit smashed him in the head.

A loud sound blurted out through the darkness as Professor Ogletree screamed when the heavy fruit exploded against the side of his temple.

Professor Dudley had groped his way between the jungle of tropical plants and fired the cannonball fruit with deadly aim at close range straight at his target. Holly saw that he had invested the throw with all his fifty years of pent-up festering disappointment and frustration at living in the shade of Professor Ogletree, uttering a primal scream that echoed through the greenhouses.

Suddenly, all went quiet.

Holly was shocked, and she didn't move a muscle and even regretted having to take tiny sips of air, lest she give away her hiding spot under the table.

She had just witnessed a crime! Assault at the least, but if Professor Ogletree didn't start moving soon, she might have to upgrade her assessment to murder! She was in the same greenhouse complex as a killer!

Oh, my gosh, Holly thought, *I am in sooooo much trouble. I can't let anyone know I was in here! If Dudley tells anyone I was his newly hired intern, they might think I was his accomplice!*

Professor Dudley kept groping his way to the bench, having hurled the cannonball fruit at where he thought Professor Ogletree sat on the bench. Dudley took out his cell phone, hit the flashlight button, and briefly lit up his victim.

Suddenly, Dudley broke out into the most maniacal laughter she had ever heard.

Ye gods, Holly thought, *he has gone legit mad.*

Apparently still in the midst of his festering anger that had not yet slacked, Professor Dudley suddenly seemed to hit upon an inspired idea.

"Ogletree, old buddy, even you would have to give me

credit about this idea I just had. It's so perfect. I can't believe no one has thought of it!" Holly watched as he proceeded to wrestle his dead rival off the bench, over the downed potted palm, and onto the circular pathway. He then dragged his body around the circular pathway and into the Rainforest Room.

Holly felt drawn to see what Dudley would do next...like a moth to a flame. She hoped she wouldn't be the one ending up getting burned.

She left her hiding spot under the table and silently pushed her way into the Tropical Forest Room. Her shoes immediately got wet from all the water on the floor from Dudley's hosing and the sprinklers.

Silently, she crossed the length of the room and hid under a table in this room now. She crouched down under it and resumed monitoring the situation while looking through a bottom window. A terrible stench started to permeate the room.

Next door in the Rainforest Room, the gigantic corpse flower was waking up from its years-long slumber and starting to open. Already, the putrid stench emanated from the gargantuan blossom.

She watched as Professor Dudley expertly sliced vertically along the entire length of the huge bloom with his penknife. It was still tightly closed up, although it would open and display its petals in only a couple of hours.

He reached his hand deep inside it, disturbing handfuls of petals, as he sought to create a hollow inside the vertically standing blossom. At three meters tall and three meters wide, the still closed-up bloom could function as a container, Holly surmised.

After creating the hollow inside the extra sturdy blossom, Professor Dudley clumsily hefted and dragged Professor Ogletree's body up the one-foot-high tile wall of the display and up and over into the hollow he created inside the monstrous corpse flower. He winced as he moved, as though he'd hurt his arm while he learned what dead weight really meant. Grimacing painfully, his anger seemed to blossom anew.

"Ow, you stupid man. You're a pain all the way up until the end!"

Even though Professor Ogletree was lean, Professor Dudley grunted from the effort of completing his task. He then turned and quickly exited the Rainforest Room.

It seemed this scene was so grandiose, so overwhelming, that Dudley seemed to think he had to leave instantly, or perhaps the events of the evening would unhinge his mind. Speeding to the Tropical Forest Room, he opened the door and walked briskly along the path again to the hose.

Standing only a few away from her, he had not seen her hiding spot under the table.

He quickly washed any remaining blood off the bench, the pathway, himself, and the screen doors, and then dragged the hose frantically into the Rainforest Room, where he doused the professor with water, spraying away any possible fiber evidence or fingerprints he may have left behind. The corpse flower responded to this drowning of water with additional growth, the petals seemingly opening before the bewildered professor's eyes.

Feeling like he had covered his tracks completely by washing away all the evidence, he went for the last time through the propped-open screen door back into the Tropical Forest Room, where he sped by her table.

She thought she heard him walk through the student nursery and hoped he had exited back out the emergency door he had propped open.

Willing her heart rate down so she could function, she blew out the breath she had been holding this past half-hour.

She decided to try to get out of there as quickly as possible and clambered out from under the table. Mesmerized by the night's disastrous events, she couldn't help but go silently into the Rainforest Room to take an up-close look at Ogletree.

As she rounded the corner of the cannonball tree and approached the corpse flower, she saw the half-slumped but fully dead Professor Ogletree. She saw that Dudley had placed a Venus flytrap plant in Professor Ogletree's mouth, which made it look like he had a large pair of green lips. As she watched, a fly, which had been circling the dead body, ventured too close to the Venus flytrap, and it suddenly snapped shut. Holly had seen enough and ran from the room as if possessed.

She ran right into the arms of Dudley, who quickly and cruelly turned her around and yanked one arm behind her back. He covered her mouth with his other hand.

"What a poor student you are. You can't follow directions well, can you? I told you to leave the greenhouses hours ago and not come back until the morning. You're coming with me now. I'm not having any witnesses to this."

Dudley marched her toward the Rainforest Room door. Holly's mind sped by at 200 mph. She looked down at a table as they exited. It was the same table from yesterday and still had William's copy of *Horticultural Digest* on it.

With a gigantic pull, she yanked her arm out of his grasp and grabbed a spray bottle filled with liquid fertilizer standing next to his magazine.

Dudley lunged around to look at her. She sprayed him viciously in the eyes with the liquid fertilizer at point blank range.

"Argggg, you horrible girl. I'll kill you!" Dudley sputtered, swiping at his eyes.

Holly ran toward the exit and grabbed some spades in a

pot at the door. Turning around and hurling them at him like knives, she tried to buy herself time to escape.

Suddenly, flashlights disturbed the darkness of the greenhouse and the Rainforest Room.

That's the police, Holly thought. *I wonder if William called them to do a security sweep? I never did get around to texting him that I locked the greenhouses. He must be beside himself with worry!*

Both Dudley and she stood still in their tracks. They both wanted to remain undetected by police.

Holly, because she was sure to be kicked out of Shellesby if she was found here in this mess, and Dudley, because he didn't want to be caught for the murder of Ogletree.

If Dudley is caught and rants to the police that she is his new intern, the police might think I could be on the hook as his accomplice for the murder as well! How, how, how did I get myself into such an insanely dangerous situation? Holly thought.

They both suddenly stood still and held their breath.

Holly stood motionlessly behind the cannonball tree, and Dudley stood motionlessly behind the corpse flower that was also now housing his victim, Ogletree.

They saw the flashlights sweep for a long time, but since the sprinklers and the lights were turned off, the greenhouse must have appeared relatively normal to the police outside. They apparently decided not to sweep around the whole building and did not see the emergency door propped open on the other side.

Dudley looked like he wanted to take this last opportunity to leave before the police might come back to do a more thorough search and left without looking back.

Wow! He must be scared I'll scream the place down and attract the cops to him! Okay, phew, if I can just leave here now without anybody seeing me, maybe I can separate myself from this disaster without getting thrown out of school.

Exhausted by trying to figure out her next moves on this

night of terror, Holly realized she had not called William as he'd asked. She had left her phone in her dorm room when she set out an hour earlier.

He was probably distraught and might come to the greenhouse himself to make sure she had locked it since he had no confirmation from Holly herself.

She decided she should leave the greenhouses immediately herself, and as she jogged to the exit, she saw something out of the corner of her eye, and it made her stand still.

Vaguely and hazily, she saw through the Tropical Forest Room's windows a very light blob on the wall of the Desert Room. Were those the campus police again with their flashlights?

Then, Holly realized it was the night-blooming cereus plant! It was opening!

She thought it a shame they were blooming unnoticed, but her heart was filled with terror, and she needed to leave.

Holly saw through a window by the door that William was running toward the greenhouse, so she quickly snuck out of the cracked door of the emergency exit. She had only stepped one foot outside when Dudley emerged from the bushes and yanked her backward toward him. His hand over her mouth, he held her cruelly fast against him. He quickly held a knife at her throat, and when William saw that, he slowed to a jog, and then stood still.

"Tell Berkeley I have her, and that if he wants her back, she'll cost $600,000."

"Berkeley hates Holly. She isn't worth a cent to him," William answered, the color draining from his face.

"Really? I couldn't have guessed."

"She's not the one you want."

"Yes, she is. She must be worth something to someone."

"Her parents have disowned her. She's only worth something to one person—me—and I only have my student intern salary here. I'm not tenured yet. It isn't much."

Holly was astounded at William's poise. She always knew he was a master at his emotions, but he was taking it to the next level here. His eyes met hers briefly, and she saw the torment in them, but then he schooled his features and addressed Dudley again.

"Give her to me."

"Why?"

"Give her to me. She's not the one you want."

Dudley held her tight for another minute.

He viciously dug around in her back pocket of her jeans and fished back out his $1,000 he had given her earlier in the night.

Dudley lowered the knife and shoved her toward William so hard she stumbled.

"Take your girl, then." He then turned and disappeared into the darkness of the night.

William grasped Holly by the shoulders.

She felt him shaking. Holly was impressed with how much he had controlled himself when it counted and negotiated her release.

"I felt my heart being ripped out of my body when I saw you. That image is burned into my retinas. I'll never forget it. God, Holly, I'm shaking like a leaf."

Holly was beyond words.

"Come, baby, let's get out of here. Let me lock up."

"William, Professor Ogletree is dead! He's in there! Dudley killed him!"

"Oh my God." He took her by the hand and quickly re-entered the greenhouse where she showed him Ogletree in the corpse flower.

"A corpse in the corpse flower, huh? God, that guy is a psychopath. Let's get out of here."

"We can't possibly be the people to break the news to the college. Ogletree isn't going anywhere for a couple of hours, and I'm done. So exhausted I can't see straight. You're staying with me tonight. I'm not letting you out of my sight until Dudley is caught."

They ran back to his Cot' in silence, and he unlocked the door and closed it behind him.

"Let's skip the shower and go to bed. The place will be crawling with cops in a couple hours, and I need a bit of sleep before I have to handle the day."

Holly didn't have to be told twice; she felt ready to drop with exhaustion and nerves herself.

She took her clothes off and climbed into bed. William followed soon after and spooned her with his arm tightly around her.

"I want you right here with me. My heart literally stopped when I saw him with that knife at your throat. Worst day of my life. By far."

Holly stayed silent, her mind reeling.

"Baby, we need to get you an alibi. Berkeley knows I was with him at the hospital with Ivy, but your whereabouts are unconfirmed for the evening."

"I know what to do. Can I borrow your phone? I'm gonna text my friend Daisy. I did her homework for her for a whole month when she broke her hand and it was in a cast and couldn't write with her left one. She owes me. She'll vouch for me that I was in the dorm, I'm certain. And she'll also take my text at 3:00 a.m., I bet."

Holly took the phone he handed her and texted quickly and waited a minute. They heard the beep of the text arriving on the phone. Holly read it. "She's down for it. She'll cover for me."

His hand tightened even harder around her.

"Thank God!"

"William?"

"Yes?"

"I can't breathe."

"Sorry." He loosened his hold and kissed her shoulder. She heard him drift off to sleep moments later.

Staring in the darkness, she knew tomorrow would be one of the worst days of her life too. With a shaky sigh, she closed her eyes and let exhaustion claim her.

CHAPTER EIGHT

*H*olly tried to stifle her tears. She didn't want to wake up William, but she felt wildly shook up still from the night before. Dawn already started breaking, and his bedroom grew brighter as the sun peeked through the blinds.

She felt his hand reassuringly smooth up and down her thigh, calming her. William sighed and gently kissed her shoulder. He let her process her emotions for a few minutes.

"Baby, I know."

That was all it took, and Holly immediately turned around, faced him, and let the storm of tears out. "It's just that the murder was so tough to witness. I felt so scared being trapped in there with him."

"I know! It must have been terrifying to you."

"It was just such an out-of-control situation. It was a train wreck, and I was caught in there like a fly in a spider web."

"I am still shaking myself. It was so traumatic. That Dudley's mind became completely unhinged, and he went on a spree of impassioned, rash actions that resulted in a murder. It's virtually impossible to process all these emotions right now. You need to get in the shower and get ready for the day. I'll take Sweetpea out and then give her some breakfast. Come, baby, be brave for me and go get ready."

As Holly turned to get out of bed, William's phone rang.

He rolled away from her and reached for it on his night-stand. "Hello? Yes, sir. She's here with me. Okay, we will see you there. Goodbye, sir."

"Berkeley?" Holly surmised.

"Yes, he wants us at the greenhouse in twenty minutes. Hurry, babe, take a quick shower. I'll have your breakfast ready when you come out." William gave her a quick kiss, and both got out of bed.

Holly took a quick shower, and William handed her one of her own freshly heated raspberry muffins on a plate.

"Holly, start your breakfast while I go and quickly get ready, then we have to talk a minute. Berkeley called back again, and he's ready to skin you alive. We will have to brain-storm a minute before we go see him. I'll be right back."

He went into the bathroom himself now to get ready, and she forced herself to take a bite or two of the muffin. She felt more scared than she had ever felt in her life. Holly always feared Director Berkeley on a good day, and this could hardly be called a good day. She closed her eyes and tried to will away the panic attack setting in.

William came out of the bathroom and sat on the bed next to her. "Okay, he called back when you were in the shower. Apparently, he was so wound up from Ivy's sleepwalking and the hospital trip that he couldn't sleep and decided to go to the greenhouse to do some paperwork to calm his mind. He said that he immediately smelled that horrible stench of the corpse flower and discovered Ogletree in there at four in the morning."

"Oh, my goodness! What else did he say?"

"He told me he called the police, and they got the body out

of the corpse flower unobserved by the rest of the campus student body because no one was up at that time. He wants to keep it that way because he is beside himself already about Ivy's sleepwalking scene. Did you know that someone filmed her last night and uploaded it to their Twitter and Facebook accounts?"

"Really? Wow. That was fast."

"Apparently, Ivy's performance has been on all the news stations, and she is an internet star now."

"I can't believe this. But I guess the internet would go crazy for something like that!"

"So, he got Ogletree's body off the campus surreptitiously and told me he wants to keep it that way. Police are crawling all over the greenhouses, but he said he is telling people a theft occurred rather than a murder."

"Is he mad at me?" Holly asked with acute dread.

"Baby, that doesn't even scratch the surface of what he feels toward you."

"What! I'm scared, William!"

"So, tell me the truth. What happened? I told you to lock up the greenhouses, and I expected you to do that the minute I left! How did you let those two professors in there?" William was angry with her now and gave her a sharp look.

"Well, you won't believe this, but Dudley accosted me the minute you left me in the Botanical Garden, and he offered me an internship with *him*. He gave me $1,000 and said the internship is mine if I just leave the greenhouse area immediately."

"Is that what he was fishing out of your pocket last night? That $1,000?"

"Yes."

"Holly! I can't believe you! You were supposed to follow my directions and tell Ogletree that the cereus blooming was off. Berkeley thinks that had you done that, none of this would have happened."

"My God! Are you suggesting this murder is all *my* fault?" Holly jumped to her feet and stood a few feet away from him, staring at him with huge shell-shocked eyes. She was beside herself with terror now.

"I'm not saying that whatsoever. Come back here, baby."

Holly stood her ground as she confronted him. "How could I possibly know this terrible nightmare would happen? I need the money! My parents disowned me, I'm here on scholarship, and I have both Ivy and her father trying to get rid of me at all times. Put yourself in my shoes! I just lost the internship with Ogletree during the Night Lights Ball, but here was a new internship opportunity. How could I turn it down? I have no money!"

She was beside herself with panic. "And anyway, it's *your* fault! If you are so clairvoyant and knew this murder was coming, why didn't you take time out of your busy schedule and take five minutes to quickly lock the greenhouses before you went to the hospital?" Holly spun away from him in utter turmoil.

William stood up, quickly went to her, and drew her in for a hug. "I don't believe any of this is your fault. You could not possibly know that Dudley was going to lose his mind. You're right—it was my responsibility. Like you, how could I know this 'one in a billion' chance that something this horrendous would happen at that exact moment? No one could have fore-seen this insanity. I'll cover for you with Berkeley. I will tell him to focus his wrath on me. It was my fault the greenhouses weren't closed."

Holly felt her trembling subside as his comforting words hit home. "Okay, please don't throw me under the bus."

"I'd sooner throw *myself* under the bus before you, Holly! Baby, nothing, I mean *nothing*, is getting between us. You and I are an inseparable team. There's no daylight between us. I love you to the ends of the earth, and I will be beside you when he grills you. I will do whatever I can with every fiber of my being."

Holly tried to stop shaking.

"Come now. It's time we go. I'll never leave you. I've got your back. Now, be brave for me and face Berkeley." He deepened his hug, seemingly trying to merge his very soul with hers. With a deep look into her eyes and a deep sigh, he turned them toward the door. He checked that Sweetpea had enough water in her bowl, then he held her hand, and they left his cottage to go to the greenhouse.

William leaned down and whispered in her ear as they walked briskly toward their doom. "You have to play dumb about the whole Dudley internship thing. You have to play dumb about witnessing the murder. There's no way for us to untangle that mess. Once they start pulling threads here and you 'fess up to his internship or something, they will try to pin this harder than ever on you. I wish I could out Dudley so they can catch him, but that starts so many other questions, and we will be backed into a corner so fast our heads will spin. I truly believe we need to play completely dumb on everything 'Dudley' and just see if we can save you from being expelled for the Ivy tea thing."

Holly nodded. "William! One more thing…"

"What is it, Holly?" William's voice sounded strained with urgency. "We have to get to the greenhouses right this minute."

"I know, but…here's the thing…I thought during the confrontation I witnessed last night between the two professors that I heard Dudley say he has the goods on the two murders. He meant that he somehow witnessed the murder of that student in Providence and the one behind the Science Building last night. He accused Ogletree of them both!"

"Wow, Holly, what a bombshell this is. Let me think for a

minute…this doesn't really change anything about our strategy, as it still would mean you have to tell the police you were in the greenhouses last night, and then they will interrogate you about Ogletree's own death. I think we stick to the plan. The plan is to save you from getting expelled right now because of the Ivy tea incident, and then we will come up with a plan to share with Berkeley about your involvement with the events of last night. Come on, we are getting very late, and he will be even angrier at you. Let's go," William directed, and they continued briskly toward the greenhouse.

Berkeley waited for them outside and ushered them in with a forbidding expression on his face.

Soon, she found herself in a conference room with William next to her on one side of a table, while the detectives, the president of the college, and Berkeley sat at the other side. The major rooms of the greenhouse were cordoned off with police crime scene tape, but the student nurseries stayed open so the college could continue to hold the regular horticultural classes in there.

"Well, we've combed the greenhouses for any possible trace evidence but so far have found none," Detective Wood said. "We saw the crime scene was completely hosed down and realize this is a wily killer who has intelligently washed away all the incriminating evidence. We don't even know if this murder is related to the body found in the back of the Science Building."

"Well, it's obviously a crime of passion. Manslaughter," said another detective. "Something so emotionally charged, it was a spontaneous crime. Those kinds of crimes always leave trace clues. I'm sure we will find something, but for now, nothing is linking Holly to either scene and her roommate vouched that she was with her in her dorm room all last night."

William turned his head minutely toward Holly. He gave

an imperceptible shake of his head, warning her not to let on to the police that she knew anything.

With a microscopic nod to him, she turned back to the detective.

"That is, unless you want to press charges about Ivy's sickening. We'd like to interview Ivy ASAP, Professor Berkeley."

"Yes, you should, but she has class right now, so it'll have to be afterwards."

Berkeley turned to the president of the college, Ms. Dahlia Jones. "Ivy was up all night at Mt. Cedar Hospital having her blood drawn, giving urine specimens, and having her stomach pumped. She was released just this morning."

Holly had been initially cleared by the police for the murder, at least in this ultra-early stage of the investigation, but Director Berkeley was beyond incensed at her serving Ivy the potent tea.

"What was their conclusion?" Dahlia asked him.

"Well, Ivy had her stomach pumped, and the contents analyzed, but the half-digested herbs they found in there were unidentifiable by the lab. As Holly just told me, they were rare herbs found only in one forgotten Louth farmer's ancient garden in England, and they weren't found in the database of the blood lab's computer."

"What do you think?" asked Dahlia.

"Well, I want to get down to the bottom of this and identify those herbs. I want to see if this is a mere a prank or something more malicious."

Dahlia nodded in agreement.

"And even worse, some of the protestors had ventured over from the science building last night."

Holly had seen this play out last night, and it still stunned her. The protestors standing outside the greenhouse had renewed their chanting of "workers before profits" and "hey, hey—ho, ho! Ogletree Chocolates have got to go!" when they saw the chocolate cascade down from the piñata at the evening's end. They were incensed when Professor Ogletree was being toasted. Holly remembered them being pushed back by campus security to the Science Center.

"Well, you won't believe this, but one of them, and I will find out who, filmed Ivy during her 'mad scene' last night. They instantly uploaded it to their social media pages, where it almost immediately caught fire, and by now, Ivy is a viral phenomenon, being described as the 'Shakespearean Sleepwalker of Shellesby.' Good God!"

Holly knew the video of Ivy spouting insanely good Shakespearean rejoinders in her wild hallucinations would attract the attention of the internet and that Shellesby College had burst into the news in the way it most hated. Controversially, and scandalously, what with the discovery of Professor Ogletree's corpse in the corpse flower and Ivy's uninhibited over-the-top performance. For an ivy-league school steeped in tradition and conservatism, this was about as bad as it could get. She knew the administrators and donors, not to mention Ivy's father, Director Berkeley, were aghast.

If they could pin any of this on her, they would.

Berkeley narrowed his eyes and swung them back in her direction. "Holly, how could you have not locked up the greenhouses? I thought I told William to tell you to lock up before we left for the hospital!"

"Sir," William jumped in instantly, "sir, this is my fault. You told me to lock up. It was my responsibility, and I delegated it to her because, sir, how on earth could any of us expect this nightmarish outcome? In reality, it should have just been another night with no intruders in the greenhouse. Please focus your wrath on me. It was my responsibility."

Berkeley gave Holly another withering look. "Go to class and get out of my sight. I am one millimeter away from pressing charges about Ivy."

"Yes, sir." She and William rose to leave.

At the door, William gently grasped her wrist.

"Hey." His voice cut like a whip, at odds with his gentle touch on her hand. Her eyes cut to him. He leaned over and whispered roughly in her ear. "Keep your head down and your mouth *closed*. Berkeley has had it with you. Don't push your luck." William gave her a warning glance.

Holly nodded, and he released her wrist, and she left the room. As luck would have it, both she and Ivy had a bonsai workshop that morning, and she knew there was bound to be a showdown soon. With a deep breath, she walked down the corridor and into the student nursery where she saw Ivy and the rest of the sixteen students waiting for class.

"It was the worst thing that's ever happened to me!" Ivy was regaling the class about her experience last night. She then caught sight of Holly and screamed, "You *poisoned* me, you little jerk!" She looked incensed past all reason.

Holly knew she had not had a peaceful slumber last night, having had her stomach pumped and all.

Her first class back was here, right back in the greenhouses, at the scene of her outrageous theatrical display only a scant few hours earlier. She now was face-to-face with Holly for the first time since her wild Bacchanalian experience and seemed eager to confront her.

"There she is, *Lucretia Borgia* herself!"

Holly and Ivy were both in World History 101, and the class had just finished a chapter on famous poisonings in world history. Lucretia Borgia was famous for her hollow ring she used to slip poison into many a drink.

"Ivy, shut up," Holly said.

"Oh, wait. Maybe it's *Catherine de Medici*! Have you come back, *Cathy*, to finish me off today?"

Holly rolled her eyes. They had also just finished studying

Catherine de Medici, who also was rumored to have poisoned many people.

"Um, my name is actually *Hol-ly*, okay, *I-vy?*" Holly said, feeling her temper start to flare.

"Okay, *Hol-ly*, but you still tried to poison me. I'll never forgive that!"

"I didn't poison you, Ivy! If I'd wanted to poison you, *believe me*, I'd have picked different herbs!"

Ivy sputtered in indignation at that insouciance.

"The ones I used were to help you enjoy a peaceful slumber. I didn't know they'd cause hallucinations. Slight miscalculation on my part. Sorry," Holly said, unrepentant and defiant.

Ivy practically stuttered she was so upset. "You, you, you...*slightly miscalculated?*" Ivy said incredulously.

Holly was dimly aware of the student nursery door opening, and she realized it must be William, and he would hear her catfight.

Who am I kidding? Holly asked herself. This was no catfight; this was World War III!

Every pent-up emotion both she and Ivy had ever had spilled out now in a torrent of words. The bonsai workshop class was due to start any minute, but the teacher was late. So, the entire class of sixteen young women stood watching raptly as the two went at it. Holly took a quick peek at William as he entered the room. He quickly made a cutting motion at his throat. Clearly, he wanted her to stop fighting with Ivy, but her temper was roused, and this come-to-Jesus with Ivy was long past due.

"I made you an internet star, Ivy! You should be thanking me! My tea was meant as a harmless sleeping draught, but apparently, it caused a few interesting hallucinations as well. You were magnificent! The best I ever saw you perform!"

Ivy stared daggers with her ice blue eyes.

"You should have seen yourself. You were a modern-day

Calliope, Greek Muse of Poetry...and Terpsichore, Greek Muse of Dance! You broke out of that fake mask that you always wear and were finally real! *Would the real Ivy please stand up?*" Holly laughed at her own joke. "You *finally* broke out of your little pristine snow globe existence and had all your fake snow shaken up for once!"

Ivy stared more daggers at her.

"You were magnificent—a complete revelation—and the internet backs me up too! All your videos have gone viral. You've been featured on the news, the 'Shakespearean Sleep-walker at Shellesby!' For goodness sake, from what I've heard, they even composed theme music when they play clips of your video on the news! You *really* know you made it big when they bother to introduce your news segment with theme music!" Holly continued, on a roll now. "You should thank me for making you famous...Well, me and the protestors who filmed you. Without them and their itchy upload fingers, the whole smashing thing would've been lost to posterity—a true loss for us all."

Suddenly, the attention of the room riveted away from her and onto the arrival of a news crew. Apparently, news crews must have their antennae out in all directions and at all times, seeming to "magically" get tips from anonymous sources constantly.

Someone had tipped them off that Ivy was back on campus, and now, in walked a very polished, well-dressed reporter, her flawless TV makeup already in place at this early hour, her hair perfectly coiffed. Her stilettos clicked sharply on the floor as she strode down the hallway and entered the student nursery, followed by a giant burly man whose face was buried in the viewfinder of a video camera with a big fuzzy microphone jutting off the top of it.

"Miss Berkeley, how are you feeling this morning? May we have a comment? How did you feel when you woke up? Have you seen footage of your video from the other night? Viewers have been commenting on our website. You are the most talked about news story we've done this year! Could we have an interview with you now?" The reporter spat out all these questions in typical rapid, machine-gun-fire delivery, accustomed as she was to get her questions in quickly before her time ran out.

"No! Ivy is not available for comment! Please leave immediately." Berkeley had heard the fighting and just entered the room after he saw the reporter arrive.

"No, please don't leave! Ivy *is* available for commenting!" Ivy chirped back, immediately countering her father's demand to leave.

All eyes, all thirty-two eyeballs of the sixteen students assembled there, followed the action back and forth, between Ivy and her father like a tennis match.

"Honey, you are still shaken up from the other night. I don't think it's wise to give any interviews right now," soothed her father, trying to regain control of this runaway situation.

"I'm fine now and ready for any interviews!" Ivy's eyes gleamed at the prospect of even more attention.

Holly bet she had probably been initially mortified by the video footage of her performance. She probably thought everyone would laugh at her and ridicule her mercilessly. So far, that hadn't seemed to have happened to her, and beyond that, Holly also wondered if her sarcastic words spoken in anger had finally penetrated her embarrassment and were starting to percolate slowly down into the layers of her encrusted confining beliefs she had of herself.

Always striving to be perfectly comported at all times, this video version of Ivy unplugged, with dirty bare feet dancing in an herb garden and spitting out Shakespearean quotes under a moonlit sky, probably had changed her whole view of herself and her tightly controlled persona she presented to the world, Holly mused.

Meanwhile, Director Berkeley returned his attention to Holly with renewed venom. He made it clear he believed that, if it wasn't for her, this whole embarrassing and appalling scene wouldn't be taking place, and there wouldn't be reporters crawling all over Shellesby trying to interview his daughter about her maniac movements last night.

"I thought I told you to shape up! I'm ready to press charges against you," Director Berkeley said, honing in on the person responsible for this debacle.

Holly again opened her mouth to speak, but with the air crackling now with tense emotion, Holly's survival instinct kicked into high gear. Pondering her next utterance carefully, realizing she was now on the thinnest ice, she started to open her mouth in her defense, when suddenly the attention of the room was riveting away from her and back to Ivy.

"No, wait! I don't want Holly to leave Shellesby just yet. I am not pressing charges, so there is no reason to have her expelled. I want to talk to her about those herbs a bit later. But I have an interview to do right now, so if you'll excuse me." Ivy gave that directive to her father as she brushed by him in the narrow confines of the student nursery and led the reporter and cameraman trailing after her in her wake, like ducklings following a mother duck. "Let's go out here in the Butterfly Garden for the interview. There's more room there, and I feel I could use a bit of fresh air right now."

She strode off majestically, the nursery now losing one-half of the historically bitter rivals. The air seemed to go out of the room suddenly with Ivy's departure, and the students filtered out as well, heading to their next class.

Berkeley turned to Holly. "You are suspended until further notice. College President Ms. Dahlia Jones told me that you are to be suspended for any additional misstep. You have *vaulted* over the line, and now you are one millimeter away from being expelled. You may clean the greenhouse and replant the herb garden—nothing else. When you aren't doing those tasks, you are to stay strictly in your dorm room."

"But, sir," William started.

Berkeley held a hand up. "You bailed her out once, but she didn't shape up. She will now take her punishment unless she wants to just pack her bags and leave right now."

"No, sir, she'll stay. Thank you."

"But, sir, I have two tests today and a paper due!" Holly protested.

"Which classes?"

"World history and chemistry."

"Good, I'll let the professors know that you are to receive a zero on them all," Berkeley said cruelly.

"But, sir," William and Holly said simultaneously.

Berkeley held up a hand. "William, I run this place. I make the rules. Holly, you are to absorb those zeros into your grade point average. If you want to get your grades up after your suspension, I'll allow them to give you the opportunity of extra credit to try to even out your average. Doing that extra work will keep you busy so you won't have time for these dramas."

"Well, thank you, sir. I do value my Shellesby education, as I see it as my stepping stone to my future. I am sorry for all the trouble I caused and will work hard to get my grades up, sir."

Holly noticed Ivy had re-entered the greenhouse and listened intently in on the conversation. Holly squirmed with embarrassment, but she had bigger worries at the moment. Receiving zeros on all these things today would plummet her average down to around a C- or a D+. She had to focus exclusively on that and decided to pay Ivy no more mind.

"William, go prune back the staghorn fern in the Fern Garden."

"Yes, sir."

"Holly, you can wash the entire greenhouse windows. There's the window cleaner." He pointed to the utility closet.

"Yes, sir."

Both Berkeleys left.

William gave a deep sigh. "You're going to have to take your punishment, baby. I tried my best for you."

"I know you did. Thank you."

"I warned you about these things, but I won't belabor the point further. Don't worry. We'll get your grades up. You'll do that extra credit. I'll make sure of that. You're grounded. I'm not taking you to any movies or date nights until the grades are back up. But I'll study with you. We can make popcorn every night after dinner and make it fun. Deal?"

"Thank you. I don't want to flunk out of here."

"Impossible! Not on my watch. You'll bounce back from this better than ever. I gotta go. Keep it together, and I'll catch up with you later."

"Thanks, William."

William left, and she was alone in the greenhouse.

Since Berkeley had assigned her to wash every window in the place, she grabbed the window cleaner and started to clean.

Holly got lost in her thoughts; her mind stayed occupied as she sprayed a paper towel down with glass cleaner and started cleaning the windows directly over the basil pots. She worked her way slowly down that entire side of the student nursery, the tightly coiled, angry energy in her hands providing quite a ferocious touch as she washed the windows. Peeling off a section of the paper towel, she'd then break it off with an angry snap before liberally spritzing glass cleaner on it in sharp, frustrated spurts. Slamming the glass cleaner bottle back down, she'd rub at a spot or two on the windows, over and over, with her mind in turmoil.

She realized she had to get a small step ladder to do the upper windows. As she walked back into the utility room, she caught sight of the bonsai trees the class was growing on the table on the right.

Haha! Holly thought. What would happen if Ivy's bonsai died of "mysterious" causes? She deserved it, Holly reckoned.

Holly felt an acute sting of regret.

Not only did she get suspended, but she'd have to resign herself to studying overtime for weeks for that extra credit just to get her grades back up. And then to top it all off, Ivy somehow became an internet star because of her hallucinations, propelling her to more of the attention she craved.

Holly felt so frustrated she couldn't bear it. She knew she couldn't vent any more to Ivy about it, but venting her frustration on Ivy's hapless bonsai was another matter.

She walked over to a small bonsai pine growing in a pretty blue and white Chinese pot. The tiny sign stuck in the dirt of the dwarf white pine tree proclaimed its Latin name *Pinus Strobus*. Underneath it was Ivy's signature. Holly liberally sprayed the small tree with the ammonia cleaner before scooping up her paper towel roll and spray bottle with a grim smile and headed out of the nursery to store the items in the utility closet. She left the greenhouse to find lunch just as Ivy finished her interview. Ivy called for her to come over.

Ye gods, will this never end? Holly thought. She realized she couldn't very well ignore her in front of the reporter and camera man. They were packing up to go, but she was sure they would pull the cameras and fuzzy microphone back out in a flash if she started arguing with Ivy again.

She had no choice but to do Ivy's bidding and go to her.

"What's up?" Holly asked Ivy as the reporter and cameraman walked down the path back to the parking lot.

Ivy imperiously informed Holly that she was now her last chance to stay in Shellesby College. "If it weren't for me and if

I'd pressed charges, you'd have already been gone half an hour ago!" Ivy said, reigniting their beef.

"Well, it's me you have to thank for your interview!" Holly retorted, the two of them locked in the most intense moment of their years-long rivalry.

Holly suddenly lost her appetite for all this drama. Her grades were slammed down into the dirt now that she was forced to miss tests. She did need to shape up now and fast. "Listen, I'm going to play it straight with you. No more games from me. I had my butt whipped pretty hard today, and I'm about done. I'm asking you to please leave me alone now so I can do my work. I'm calling a ceasefire."

Ivy looked at her, stunned.

"Well, I have one better. I'm calling a truce."

Holly's eyebrows shot up to her hairline. "A truce?" She narrowed her eyes with suspicion.

"Well, it's as you say...I am shocked and appalled at the video, yet I can't stop watching it. Is that me? I vaguely remember some of it, but most of it seems like a dream to me, one that is hazy and patchy. I see the herb garden over there and can't believe I destroyed it! Yet the dancing was so unreal I want to experience it all again! Yes, yes, yes. You must brew me another cup, only this time not quite as strong. I want to experience it all again!"

Holly was flabbergasted. "No, never! It was a mistake. It was supposed to be a sleeping draught, but obviously, it has more potent properties than I imagined it had. I certainly am not going to ever brew that up again!"

Ivy was crestfallen as she had set her heart on trying that experience again. Only perhaps the next time, the effect would be milder based on a lower dose of the herbs the second time around.

Holly stared at Ivy as if just seeing her for the first time. She saw a confused and startled young woman who had gotten a glimpse of her potential and was unsure how to begin exploring the completely new terrain of this new side of her she just discovered last night. In that moment, she felt a connection to Ivy. After all, wasn't she also trying to emerge from her chrysalis and spread her butterfly wings in new directions too?

As this revelation dawned on Holly, she was hit by a completely wild idea. The phrase "if you can't beat 'em, join 'em" came to mind, and she wondered if the best chess move she could now make at Shellesby was to befriend her long-time rival.

Keep your friends close; keep your enemies closer.

"A truce, huh?"

"Yes."

"You mean we're going to *deactivate* the nuclear arsenal?"

Ivy laughed. "*Especially* the nuclear arsenal."

"Well, if that's true, then you can help me replant the herb garden. It's a total mess, what with you stomping your heart out in there all night long! And if you're so interested in freeing your creativity, there is an improvisation dance class that I take in the gymnasium. You could come along if you want. We do the same thing you did when you danced in the herb garden, but no plants get harmed in the process!"

"What? I've never heard of this dance class!"

"There's a live musician who provides improvised music, and the instructor leads you through guided imagery, and you just move as the mood strikes you. I think there might even still be a remnant of that full moon tonight, and I can ask the instructor if we can move the class outdoors tonight. She sometimes holds the class in the meadow by the lake on warm nights. Then, you'll be able to dance by the light of the silvery moon again, Terpsichore."

Ivy's eye lit up at this; a whole new branch of study just opened up to her. "I want that! I...uh...I feel like I have an over-tight skin on, and I have to slither out of this old skin and step into a new one. Do you...um...do you understand?"

"I do, actually."

"I'll be at that dance class tonight. Should we start replanting the herb garden for a few hours after lunch?"

"Well, *I'll* be in there by three, replanting the tender shoots after *someone* I know stomped on them like a herd of elephants!" Holly joked, feeling back in control of her destiny now that her personal Sword of Damocles, the imminent threat of expulsion, had passed her by.

"I'll be here at three p.m. too."

"Wow. Okay. That's a lot to absorb in one morning, but hey, let's do this thing!"

"Three p.m.!"

"Okay, see ya!" Holly watched Ivy walk back to her dorm. Holly then went in search of William.

She found him in a different student nursery than the one they were in earlier. Holly opened the door to the nursery and was staggered by the most noxious, strong, fishy smell permeating the room. "William, I thought we work at a greenhouse, not a fish market! What is going on?"

William laughed. "It's this new brand of fishmeal I'm using. It's a strong source of organic nitrogen." He went on to say that it stimulates vigorous growth and was uniquely processed to retain maximum nutritional value for the plants. "Now that Night Lights is finished for another year, I can nurture them with this and other fertilizers."

The small room stinking to high heaven, Holly never before understood the importance of the screen doors separating the rooms as much as she did right now. All this malodorous activity was going on just steps away from the prime Tropical Forest Room, yet visitors could remain blissfully unaware of this stench, with the trusty west screen door holding at bay this nauseating cloud of fish odor.

"How can you stand it in here? I am ready to amputate my nose in a second."

"Oh, it's nothing!" William insisted with a laugh. "It's the same as when a baker doesn't smell the scent of baking bread anymore because he smells it all day...except this smell I have to cope with sure does assault my nose for the first few minutes when I come in each morning. After that, the brain stops paying attention to a constant smell, and I am fine again."

"I don't think my nose will ever be fine again," Holly announced with surety.

"Yes, it will. One or two whiffs of my fresh veggie lasagna tonight will cure your nose in a jiffy."

"Lasagna!" Holly was ecstatic at the thought. William was a fantastic cook, and his veggie lasagna was her favorite. She even asked him to cook it for her on her birthday last year. He was obviously trying to comfort her from her tongue-lashing she took earlier today.

"Yes, dinner at my place tonight. I know Berkeley wants you on a bread and water diet in your dorm, but I'll cover for you if he finds out. I do have a little pull around here...though not limitless, as you found out today."

"Yes, that's very true, and I am certainly chastened at the moment."

William pretended to call her on a cell phone. "'Ello? I'm Vill-i-am, ze concierge from *ze* Cot' rest-au-rant," he said in a faux European accent. "I am confirming *ze din-ner* reservation for 7:00 p.m. tonight *vor ze* Miss Holly Dolly. Can *ve* count on seeing you tonight at *ze* usual table, miss?"

Holly laughed and threw her arms around William. "You are priceless and irreplaceable. I am the luckiest girl in Boston, and that's a fact."

She turned to go and then remembered her real reason for coming to find him. Now that she whipsawed this morning and was friends with Ivy, she felt a pang of guilt for having drowned her bonsai in window cleaner. "Oh, I just remembered," Holly said and suddenly started squirming a bit.

"Yes?"

"William, um…I was wondering…that is…"

"What? You've got my antennae up now. No more trouble!"

"No, no…nothing…really."

"Holly!"

"No, it's okay…it's just that I *may* or may *not* have…um… drowned Ivy's bonsai with…um…window cleaner." Holly finished the sentence in a rush.

William laughed. "Whew, at least it's not that big a thing. Oh gosh, you got my heart rate up there for a moment, baby. Okay, so did you drown her bonsai, or are you not sure?"

"Well, like I said. I *may* or may *not* have done it."

William laughed again. "Well, my money is on you *did* do it, so what do you want now?"

"Um…to reverse the damage…if possible?"

"Where there's a Will, there's a way. Show me her bonsai, and I'll see what I can do."

She led him back to the nursery she had been in and pointed out Ivy's plant.

"Well, the ammonia in the window cleaner will have thrown off the ph in the soil, but lucky for you, I aced chemistry in school, so I'll whip up a solution that will rebalance that poor little plant's ph. It should survive your machinations…if only the rest of us were so lucky."

Holly had to laugh at the truth of that. "Awesome! Thanks! I'll be at your Cot' for dinner tonight!"

"Bye, baby."

CHAPTER NINE

*I*f the college was a beehive of activity, then Ivy was Shellesby's resident Queen Bee, and her new favorite worker bee, Holly, toiled in the garden as she listened to Ivy drone on about how topsy-turvy this had all turned out.

Holly suddenly sang the "Tea for Two" song, making Ivy explode in laughter. Impulsively, she grabbed Ivy's hand, and they cha-cha'd to the music. "Tea for two, and two for tea. You for me, and me for you."

They both collapsed on the ground laughing.

"Whew," said Holly. "How many years have we been at war?"

"Um…I think the first skirmish started back in grade school, but we've been at the nuclear level for at least two years now, I think."

"That's when William came to study here," Holly noted.

"Yes."

"Well, I certainly don't want to put the nuclear arsenal back in jeopardy, but before we become best friends forever, I have something I want to say to you. Back off William. He's my… um…my *sugar* maple."

Ivy laughed. "He sure does have that *sugary* little drawl in his voice, a real Southern gentleman. Where's he from?"

"Georgia."

"Uh huh. A peach. I knew it. Listen, I'm finished with William. I have seen how he looks at you. Every girl at Shellesby is jealous of you. We all want him."

"Yes, but he's *mine*, and you really need to back off."

"I am…and don't worry. The nuclear arsenal is still deactivated."

Holly laughed.

"So, let's watch my video!" Ivy said.

Holly got her phone out and searched YouTube for Ivy's video.

"So, tell me again! What did you think? Were you laughing? Which part was your favorite? Mine was '*et tu, brute!*' " Ivy said as she collapsed laughing.

"I can't even! That was the best part! I almost peed my pants!" Holly said as she gave herself over to a fit of giggles. "I couldn't believe you said that, but it was *so* funny!"

"I know! It's my favorite part too! I can't stop watching it!" Ivy screamed, laughing uproariously.

They knelt together, sitting back on their heels in the herb garden as Holly held her cell phone for both to see as they replayed Ivy's performance. They both wore faded jeans and a short tank top with the Shellesby insignia on it.

"*Et tu, Brute?*" Ivy could be heard saying in the video when the EMTs tried to soothe her, approach her, and lead her back to the stretcher. They had approached her from behind as Ivy stared into the greenhouses at that time, so her perfectly timed quote just maximized the comedic effect.

"And, and, and…look…right there…look at your expression. Oh my gosh! You look like a fierce she-wolf protecting her brood or something. I was checking to see if you also grew *fangs* as well as sleepwalked! It's too funny!" Holly sputtered with laughter as Ivy continued on in the video, saying to the hapless EMTs as they approached her:

"*Get thee to a nunnery!*"

Both women now exploded with laughter, elbowing each other as they gave in to complete zany mirth, snorting and crying, as tears streamed down their cheeks from their intense jollity.

"Wait, wait, wait…Watch this…Let's replay that…Watch…Wait…*Right here…*" Holly was almost incoherent with glee as she replayed the scene again. Again, Ivy's ferocious visage was seen as the video was rewound to the same spot. This time, Holly didn't pause the video but let the scene play out. "*Et tu, Brute? Get thee to a nunnery!*" And the two women fell over into the dirt at the preposterous sight of the sleepwalking Ivy.

"I don't even remember saying that!" Ivy said, tears streaming down her cheeks. She wiped them away with the back of her hand, leaving a small dirt smudge streak across her nose.

"Let's watch your dance number! It really was rather amazing, if I do say so myself!"

Holly fast forwarded the video playing on her cell phone to the section where Ivy trampled the herbs down in the garden. "Watch how you reach your arms slowly upwards as if trying to touch the moon. You were rather graceful, though. I think you'll love improv dance class tonight!" Holly said as Ivy sat in the dirt, riveted on the cell phone, watching her image dancing in the herb garden under the moonlight.

"Did you enjoy dancing barefoot last night?"

"It's the best thing! I vaguely remember it. I think my feet were getting quite dirty, and the stones in here were poking me quite a bit!" Ivy grimaced in remembrance.

"Well, it *is* a garden, silly! It has stones in it! But we'll leave no stone unturned now as we try to even out the soil again, and then we can get to the replanting of the herbs. Here, start raking the soil over in that patch." Holly pointed to a clump of soil that had been upturned during Ivy's nighttime performance. Sticking her phone into her back jeans pocket, Holly picked up another rake and started on an adjacent patch.

The soil well-tilled now, Holly directed Ivy to grab one of the trays of tiny herb seedlings that Holly had prepared in the student nursery an hour ago. Filled with tiny versions of basil, peppermint, oregano, thyme, and chives, the two women dug out a seedling from the tray and planted it in the ground in segregated rows, separating each herb. They knelt there, on all fours, crawling around on the ground as they did this, resembling toddlers in the "cruiser" stage of development.

They repeated this over and over until the entire segment of the garden Ivy had trampled was once again planted with herbs, though these little seedlings would take weeks to grow to the size of the former plants.

Holly brushed the dirt off her hands as she stood up and directed Ivy to drag the garden hose over to water the newly planted seedlings.

"Wow! I am *impressed*! Good as new. Did it feel cathartic to help with the replanting?"

"You know, it reeeeally did. I'm glad you asked me to help."

"Come on! It's a super hot day today, and you must be parched. Come with me, and we'll have a little iced tea in the Visitor's Center kitchen."

"Are you *kidding* me?" Ivy screeched in bewilderment. "I've had enough of your *teas*, thank you very much." Ivy had to laugh despite herself.

"Relax, Ivy. I make a fresh pitcher of herbal tea each day for the Science Building staff. It's a communal pitcher, so it's perfectly safe—I assure you. I'll drink from it first to prove it to you!"

Ivy laughed. "Well, okay, if you drink it first!"

They both walked out of the herb garden, and Holly held

open the door for them to enter the Visitor's Center. She led the way to the kitchen and retrieved the pitcher from inside. Pouring herself a glass of her homemade peppermint and lavender iced tea, she drained it quickly, and then turned to Ivy with an innocent smile. "See? Nothing to worry about!"

"Well, okay, then I'll take a glass too. Thanks," Ivy said politely.

After she poured Ivy's glass and watched her take the first sips, Holly dramatically spun on her heel and grasped her throat tightly.

"Oh, I was wrong! This is the tainted tea! Oh, my goodness, I gave you the wrong one!" Holly kept up the theatrics as she spun around and bent in half and pretended to cough up half a lung. She put her hand to her forehead and made noises as if she were dying. "To be or not to be! That is the question!" Holly pretended to sleepwalk and held her arms out in front of her, parodying Ivy from the night before.

Ivy laughed so hard she sputtered and spewed iced tea all over the countertop.

"What drama! You missed your calling as an actress!"

Both girls laughed companionably and even polished off another glass due to being parched from their hard exertions from the planting.

"Okay, now that we aren't thirsty anymore, come with me to my office. We have to talk about a few things."

"*Office*? You have an office?" Ivy asked incredulously.

"I do indeed. Come." Holly led the way back outside and strode toward the Butterfly Garden. She held the tall bushes aside like holding a door open for Ivy.

"Welcome to my office. It's the best one on campus!"

Ivy laughed and entered the Butterfly Garden. Holly led them to the secluded inner area and spread a blanket down to try to avoid tick bites.

"There, no one can see or hear us way over here in the thicket of grasses and flowers," Holly explained.

After they were both settled cross-legged on the blanket, Holly gave a deep sigh.

"So, here's the thing. Did you hear about the murder last night?"

"*Murder*? No! Oh my goodness, what happened?"

Holly looked intently at Ivy. "Well, it's as I suspected, even your father didn't want you to know about it. He has kept the whole thing totally under wraps. Professor Ogletree was murdered last night in the greenhouse!"

"Oh my goodness! I can't believe it! But…how?"

"Listen, I expect you to not breathe a word about all this to *anyone*. Understand?"

"How do *you* know about it?"

"Well, I am William's girlfriend, and he knows about it too. I wanted to let you know that so you can process that information by yourself and not be blindsided by hearing it from someone else."

"I can't even wrap my mind around that right now," Ivy said with bewilderment.

"Well, looks like you lost your internship. You were cruel to me last night, though! You know I need that financial help. I don't have money as you do, and you were a real jerk to me last night!"

"Well, takes one to know one! You tried to trip me with that ridiculous horse chestnut seed pod. Had you ever thought that I could've actually fallen and possibly hit my head on the cement pathway? You would have gotten thrown out of Shellesby so fast your head would spin!"

Holly nodded in agreement. "I think we were both heedless and took things too far. I am sorry for all that and glad we could bury the hatchet…and the nuclear arsenal."

Ivy smiled in agreement.

"I'm still very shaken up about last night, though, with Professor Ogletree. Some other brutal stuff also went on, but I am still processing it all and don't want to divulge further."

Ivy looked at her with compassion. "I understand. I am mind-blown myself at the moment."

"Well, I guess we better go. I have to go take a shower before dinner with William." Holly got up and shook off the blanket, folded it, and put it under her arm. She led Ivy back to the Butterfly Garden exit and turned to her. "Okay, it was a great afternoon's work. I'm also glad we could talk a bit. Meet me by the cafeteria at eight. I'll escort you to our dance class. Wear yoga pants and a comfortable blouse."

"Me too, Holly. Great! See you then." Ivy turned and walked back to her dorm.

Holly headed to her dorm for a shower before dinner. Her stomach growled in anticipation of William's veggie lasagna. All this replanting made her famished. She went into her dorm and was in the shower in minutes. Letting the spray wash away all the dirt of the day, she tried to process the idea that she and Ivy, former mortal enemies, were now friends.

Truth is stranger than fiction, Holly thought.

CHAPTER TEN

*H*olly changed into a comfortable blouse and yoga pants since she was going to go to the evening dance class right after supper at William's. She washed her hair, as she was worried about any possible stink from that fish emollient encounter earlier in the day. With her hair still drying, she walked off campus and, five minutes later, was at his Cot' and opened the door.

"Holly, dinner's on the table. Sit down."

"Wow, my nose is having a moment! You have raised my nose from the dead. I had to wash my hair to make sure I got that entire stink out."

William came to smell her hair. "Well, you did a great job. All I smell is honeysuckle and lavender."

"Please serve me the biggest portion you can. I'm so hungry after all the drama today."

He chuckled and put half the pan of lasagna on her plate and watched her gorge herself on his tasty cooking. "So, I went to your world history professor this afternoon and begged him to let you get started on your extra credit."

"You did?"

"Yes, because you'd better take this seriously at this point. Shellesby is a very competitive school, and the administration does review grades every quarter, and Berkeley may have almost checkmated you here. If you are not thrown out for your antics, you will be for your poor grades."

"I know! I see the light. I'm scared to death about my GPA at this point."

"Not to worry. Not only did I beg him to let you get a start, but I helped him pick a topic for you. He was all ready to assign you a big paper about the feudal system in eleventh century Europe, but I convinced him to assign a more exciting topic. Feast your eyes on these!" He gestured to a large stack of books on the coffee table in front of the sofa. They were two inches thick and had *Galapagos Islands* on the spine.

"William! I am a junior. I am not going for my Ph.D.! Those books are monstrous!"

William laughed. "Noooo, those are for me. I love looking at pictures of those islands. The smallest one is for you. I got him to change the topic to the Galapagos Islands, which is a much more interesting topic than eleventh century feudal Europe! And best yet, I did my master's thesis on the Galapagos, so I'm an expert on the place and can help you study. You're in good hands with me!"

And with that, he walked around to her seat and gently pulled her upright. He then cupped her face with his left hand to give her a quick kiss while simultaneously tickling her ribs with his right hand.

She was so busy reacting to his gentle assault on her lips and ribs she didn't know if she was coming or going.

He finished with a friendly squeeze of her hand.

"As I said, you are in *good* hands with me. *Literally.*"

Holly was in love with his strength. He really knew how to handle her. A few years older than her, he was much more mature than Holly, but he was so gentle with her that she didn't feel the age difference at all.

"William, I never know what you're doing from one minute to the next!"

"I feel the same way about you, baby, trust me. However, I do know what we are going to do in *these particular* next few minutes. We're studying!

"To the couch," William ordered. "Start cracking open that book and read. I'll make us popcorn and gather Sweetpea, and we should settle down for at least an hour to help you chip away at your mountain of work."

"Agreed!" And she went to the couch to start.

After an hour, she decided to try to persuade him that it was time to go. After all, she still had the evening dance class to attend.

Yawning, she said, "I am so tired. I better go."

"Good idea." He walked her over to the door. "I have a big day tomorrow—I'm tackling the golden barrel cactus and going to transplant it to a larger vat. That'll take a couple of hours."

"Thoughts and prayers, William."

William grinned. "Goodnight. Love you, babe."

Holly briskly left his Cot', headed back to campus, and walked in the direction of her dorm.

Once she was sure she was out of his line of sight, she made a sharp u-turn and headed to the lake. She didn't want William to know about this dance class because she bet it probably wasn't on Berkeley's list of allowable activities during her suspension.

She imagined Daphne, the dance instructor, would move the class outside tonight. The air was so clean and fresh without a single drop of chill.

She swung by the cafeteria to see Ivy looking pretty in a nice blouse and yoga pants.

"You're a little late! I thought you weren't coming," Ivy said.

"Oh, I just couldn't break away, but I'm here now. Come this way. I sure it's outdoors tonight."

"Really?"

"Probably. Let's go!"

They walked in companionable silence for a few minutes.

Ivy suddenly broke the silence and asked, "What exactly did you serve me at the Night Lights Ball?" She squinted at Holly in the darkness as she tried to scan Holly's expression for any sign of malevolence.

"Relax! I wasn't trying to poison you! I just wanted to discuss the internship with Ogletree without you nosing around, so I intended for you to drink a sleeping draught and go back to your dorm and sleep it off. I had hoped to get that internship because your father threatened to revoke the scholarship I have here!" Holly explained.

"Well, now neither of us is going to get an internship," Ivy said, shuddering at the memory of poor dead Professor Ogletree. "Show me the herbs you used, though. I'm so curious!"

"They got trampled underfoot by you, silly!" Holly hedged.

"Oh," Ivy said crestfallen. "I just wanted to see them for myself."

Feeling a budding kinship with Ivy— after all, she had helped her remain here at Shellesby—Holly had a change of heart. If it wasn't for Ivy's intervention, Director Berkeley would've expelled her already.

"Well, okay. We're already late. A little longer probably won't matter. Come! Let's quickly jog to the herb garden, and I'll show you."

Three minutes later, they stood at the newly planted herb garden, so she led Ivy to the far side of the patch, the uppermost northeast corner. Ivy hadn't gone that far with her dancing last night, so they were still intact and unharmed.

"Here they are. I call them Friar Lawrence herbs." Holly giggled as she recalled last night.

"Friar Lawrence herbs?" Ivy struggled to understand. "You mean *Friar Lawrence*, Friar Lawrence, of *Romeo and Juliet* fame?"

"The one and the same!" Holly confirmed.

"You were trying to put me in a coma that resembled death?" Ivy shrieked, instantly alarmed and suddenly worried that her new bestie was trying to kill her.

"Relax! It was a sleeping draught—nothing more! I was intrigued last fall when we performed *Romeo and Juliet* because I was already working here in the greenhouses and tending the herb garden. I was just fascinated as to which herbs they might be, so I Googled 'Friar Lawrence herbs' and found these! The farmer never mentioned anything about hallucinations or things like that!" Holly explained. "Believe me, I was more surprised than you were when you started hallucinating!"

"Wow." Ivy had become overwhelmed by this new onslaught of information. "Friar Lawrence herbs. Are you kidding me? *Who Googles Friar Lawrence herbs?*"

Ivy's imagination was now stimulated, and she imagined an elderly farmer in the middle of nowhere, England, growing these renaissance herbs that dated back to the Bard himself. She burst out laughing.

"Let's harvest a few and brew another pot of tea! I want to try it again, though perhaps a weaker dose!"

"No! Absolutely not!" Holly had had enough drama, theatrical and otherwise, for the time being. She just wanted to lie low and let the accusations and suspicions die down.

"Okay. I was just curious—that's all. Should I come back here tomorrow and water again?" Ivy inquired, seemingly loathed to break the connection she felt she was forging with her former arch-nemesis.

"Yeah, I'll be here weeding the garden, and you could help water if you want." Holly smiled, accepting the olive branch. "You have a lot more in you than your fake surface persona lets on, you know."

"Fake surface persona?" Ivy was insulted that anyone would call her that.

"Yeah, fake surface persona. When I watched you perform Juliet last fall, I could have fallen asleep each night while you performed. And I didn't even need Friar Lawrence herbs to fall asleep, either—you were so unbelievably *bo-ring*!" Holly decided to share.

"Boring?" Ivy was truly insulted now.

"Yup, boring! However, you seemed like a totally different person when under the influence of my tea, and for the first time, I wanted to watch you perform…Actually, you had the audience riveted on you," Holly continued on. "That level of real emotion, the changes in the inflection of your voice, the power, the drama, the passion, the intensity, all that…For the first time, you seemed like a real person to me, able to feel deep emotions, not cosseted and cocooned in your own little world. Hell, that's even why you got to play Juliet in the first place! Because you're the director's daughter, for crying out loud" Holly decided to let the dam break, and all the pent-up resentment of Ivy's preferential treatment all these years came pouring out in a torrent of words.

Ivy just stood there, looking stunned.

"But for the first time that night, I saw you express real emotion and genuine feeling. Enough that I'd even pay to purchase a ticket to see you perform." Holly snorted at that last admission. "It's too bad you're so encased in your fake persona most days that it takes a special tea for you to project and express real emotion and feeling. I feel sorry for you—that you think you can't be your real self in your daily life," Holly concluded, hoping she hadn't entirely crushed the olive branch that Ivy had just earlier extended toward her.

Ivy stayed silent through all of this and then abruptly turned and walked a few feet away.

Holly watched her walk away and, when she got to the end of the herb garden, called out softly, "I think you're going to be just fine. I think it's the beginning of finding out who you really are."

Ivy stiffened and paused as she took this in. It appeared that having Holly, whom she'd always looked down upon, become like a mentor to her and suddenly dispense advice, criticize her, and find her wanting was a lot to take in all at once.

"Well, that's a lot to think about."

"Well, Ivy, aren't we friends now?"

Ivy nodded.

"Well, friends tell each other the truth. Like when you tell your friend she has spinach stuck in her teeth. It's the same thing."

Ivy burst out laughing. "Since when were you this funny?"

"All along. It's just that our nuclear arsenal got in the way. Come on! We're soooooo late."

She led the way, and they both jogged to the meadow by the lake and joined the class way in the back. Daphne gave her a wave, and the rest of the students looked around once, and then continued with their class.

The class was listening to a poem Daphne read.

It was a Japanese haiku, only five lines, and then she asked the class to meditate on it, encouraging each dancer to step away from the mundaneness of their day and become swept away with a magical landscape, the water's edge of Lake Tupelo in the evening. The swans and other waterfowl that lived on the lake glided along under the huge full moon. The class used live music as accompaniment.

"That's Ankur, Daphne's favorite musician," Holly whispered to Ivy. "He just came back from his tour of India and Hong Kong."

Ivy looked riveted by the soulful deep sounds Ankur coaxed out of his cello. A light breeze tickled the surface of the water, and the gentle lapping of the waves of Lake Tupelo provided an almost hypnotic effect on the dancers.

"Watch Daphne. She's the best! She was with the Martha Graham Dance Company for a decade as their lead dancer!" Daphne now led the improvisation, reacting instinctively to Ankur's magical music. She would bend and stretch and bow to the right and left, forward and back, arms reaching overhead and snaking around to swing down to the ground again, as the torsos of the dancers twisted and leaned, using every plane of motion to describe in movement the stirrings of their souls. Daphne would suggest a movement sequence in response to the music, and the dancers would follow and add their interpretations and movements.

Ivy danced very woodenly without any of the grace of the previous night.

"Ivy," Holly whispered, "you need to let go! Dance like... um...well, like no one is watching."

That got Ivy to sputter in laughter as she remembered just *how many* people had indeed watched her dance performance yesterday.

She tried to loosen up a bit but was completely inhibited by a seeming boatload of insecurities now that she didn't have the loosening effects of the tea Holly gave her yesterday.

They danced a few more minutes, and then the class ended. The dancers applauded as Daphne took a bow, and then they cheered and stomped to acknowledge Ankur as he stood up with his cello.

Holly turned to Ivy. "Whew, girl. Whew." Holly looked at her intently. "We're going to have our work cut out to try to liberate you from that stiffness you've encased yourself in. You are practically mummified in there with the weight of everyone's expectations of you, it seems."

"It's a lot harder without the Friar Lawrence herb tea, I can tell you," Ivy agreed.

"Don't worry." Continuing now in her new position as mentor to Ivy, Holly said, "I'll be your new life coach."

Ivy laughed. "Life coach? How many clients do you have, anyway?"

"You're my first!"

Ivy laughed again.

"Listen, it's been a reeeeally long day. Let's say goodbye, and I'll see you in the herb garden tomorrow for watering and weeding. Deal?"

Ivy agreed.

Holly tentatively reached her arms out as if she was about to embrace the golden barrel cactus.

"Well, what do you think? Are we going to do this thing?"

Ivy reached her arms out, too, and they tentatively embraced until it became a friendly hug.

"Whew! A hug from Ivy, a previous mortal enemy for the last sixteen centuries. Will stranger things ever be?"

Ivy laughed. "You are sooooo funny! Goodnight!" She turned and went down the path away from the lake and back to her dorm.

Holly waited a few minutes in the back until Daphne had said her goodbyes to her other students. She wanted to let Daphne know who Ivy was, and she always stayed late for a few minutes chatting with Daphne, as they were good friends.

As she waited, she suddenly got a little prickle of apprehension. She didn't know what it was, only that something felt off. Holly strained her ears to see if it was a sound that made her uneasy, but she couldn't identify anything amiss.

She looked at the path Ivy had just walked.

Holly couldn't shake the prickle. She walked down the path a little and looked into the bushes, but the bushes seemed undisturbed, and everything looked normal.

Daphne had finished with the other dancers now, so Holly went up to her for a couple of minutes to chat and to tell her about Ivy.

Eventually, she said goodbye to Daphne.

Turning back to her dorm, Holly felt the earlier apprehension grow until she almost felt a panic attack coming on. This time, she went along the path Ivy had taken and decided to wade deep into the bushes. She almost stepped on a tiny bunny while it hid in the bushes and ate its dinner.

Scared, the rabbit shot out of the bushes, and Holly screamed. "Whew. Only a rabbit."

Still unnerved by this feeling, she decided to get back to her dorm in a hurry.

She got ready for bed and still felt unsettled.

Holly got her phone and searched for tomorrow's horoscope.

Gemini: "Worst day of your life tomorrow. Even worse than today, if possible. Book a ticket out of town and stay there until Saturday. Otherwise, stay in bed for *real* this time."

Holly's eyes popped out.

With this *horror-scope* in her mind, she lay down rigidly in bed. She doubted she'd sleep now. Closing her eyes, she dreaded tomorrow.

I have to stop reading my horoscopes, she vowed and tried to will herself to sleep.

CHAPTER ELEVEN

he next day, Holly stared at the note taped to the greenhouse door. She snatched it off and ran to hide in the Butterfly Garden as she read it.

Her hands shook like leaves, and she felt her heart miss a beat.

I'm having a heart attack, Holly thought.

A brutal migraine descended upon her, and she closed her eyes for a minute.

Thank God she had found this while William was still at lunch. If he'd seen this, her world would have ended there right on the spot.

Shaking so hard she could hardly hold the note, she opened her eyes and read it again.

I have Ivy Berkeley. She is unharmed. Sort of. Berkeley, I'm giving you until tomorrow at dawn to send the ransom money. Ivy costs $600,000. Leave it at the tallest pine tree at the back of the lake path. You know the one.

If the money isn't there at dawn tomorrow, Ivy is dead. She's of no more use to me then, and she'll be evaporated from this earth.

P.S. don't bother bringing the police with you. I can see the pine tree from where I am. If I see any police, I'll shoot her dead in a millisecond. Here's Ivy's signature.

Holly saw Ivy's signature on the letter and knew it was legit. She had seen Ivy sign her name that way all through high school. She curved the Y in her first name to join the Y in her last name. That was Ivy's signature on the note, she was sure of it.

Holly heard William chatting with a few groundskeepers as he made his way back to the greenhouse after lunch.

"Oh, no! I've gotta hide!" Holly exclaimed.

She stuffed the note into her back pocket, then expertly climbed a large nearby tree and sat on a branch about seven feet up from the ground. She was quite hidden from view this way.

Holly sat on the branch and mentally excoriated herself.

This is all my fault! Wow! I should have never taken Ivy to that evening dance class.

Rabbit? My foot! That was not only just a rabbit in the bushes! Ivy must have been kidnapped right then. But how? I was just steps away from her when I heard that weird rustling in the bushes. I am sooooo creeped out that someone was watching us, and now she's gone! Oh my goodness, I have to get her back!

This turn of events devastated Holly, and she felt a burden of guilt descend on her, threatening to crush her.

"I'll get her back. I'll rescue her. As long as I get her back, I'll be able to forgive myself. Otherwise, I will despise myself forever! I was so stupid! The cover of darkness was just playing into his hands. Damn it! Why am I so stupid? Or is it William's fault? It's *his* fault…He kept saying, 'She's not the one you want,' when Dudley held me hostage. He was *practically mentioning Ivy by name when he said that—this is his fault! Oh my goodness!*" Holly was disgusted with herself and realized she had to think more about this, but the more she thought about it, she knew she had to call Heather.

She rang Heather's cell phone and waited.

"I'd love to come now, but this is the worst time possible. I'm at Boston Botanical Gardens now, meeting with their director. They're doing a major renovation and will have to temporarily remove their orchid collection. I told them I'd be thrilled to care for their orchids down at National Botanical Gardens until their renovation is completed. We're working out shipping details at this very moment."

"Trust me—I get the magnitude of that. I am sooooooo sorry, but I'm suspended, and Berkeley disabled my student ID swipe card, so I can't get into the library. I need to study something in there, and it's literally a life-or-death moment for me."

"I can't believe this."

"I am begging you. Please come and help me get into the library!" Holly was shrieking now.

"Geesh! Okay, okay. Calm down. I'm making my excuses, and I'll be there in an hour. Meet you in front of the library at 3:00 p.m."

"Thank you! Thanks a million!"

"Uh huh. See you soon."

Holly's mind sped by at 200 mph trying to make sense of this. She distilled it down to a few variables as she reasoned with herself. "Number one, I can't let William or Berkeley know. That much is certain. They'd hit the roof and immediately charge in with the police if they knew.

"Number two, speaking of the police...hmm...If Dudley said in his note that he can see the tallest pine tree at the edge of the lake, then he must be holding Ivy hostage on campus!

"But of course, he is," she realized. "There might be a warrant out for his arrest for the murder of Professor Ogletree, anyway, so he wouldn't be at his hotel room," she reasoned. "That means he must be somewhere on campus with Ivy. But where?"

Holly knew there were a few abandoned structures on the sprawling 600-acre campus. Shellesby College had undergone many massive renovations in its 160 years, and she knew some buildings had been abandoned from earlier eras in the college's history.

She needed Heather, and she needed the library.

And she had to get into the library undetected. Berkeley had given strict instructions that she stay in her dorm room during her suspension.

She climbed down from the tree and set out toward the library. Holly felt like a cloak-and-dagger cartoon character as she dashed from one set of bushes to the next, hiding her way across campus until she reached the library and hid in the bushes to the left of the front door.

Soon, she saw Heather walking up the path.

Holly whispered loudly, "Hey, Heather, I'm right here."

Heather looked around with a frown, and then spotted Holly crouched behind the boxwoods near the door.

"Why are you hiding in the bushes?"

"Well, I'm suspended and can't leave my dorm room."

"Well, now that I'm here, you're safe with me. I'm a mega-donor here, a pretty important alumna. You're safe with me around."

"Thank you, thank you. I can't thank you enough."

Heather used her alumna ID swipe card, and they entered the library.

"Hi," Holly said, "we are interested in any old maps of Shellesby College that you might have?"

The librarian said, "Go to the microfiche room. Maps like that are all on microfilm."

"Thank you," Holly said, and she and Heather went into the microfilm room, which happened to be empty. Heather closed the door and exploded, though she kept her voice down because it was a library.

"Old maps? What's going on? Are you in trouble?"

"I…I…I…just…"

"*What?* Just tell me what trouble you're in!"

"Um, I need to know if there are any abandoned buildings on Shellesby's campus."

"For what? I really don't like the sound of this. You have no business sniffing around abandoned buildings, young lady. What is going on?"

"I…I…I…just…Oh, Heather." Holly burst into tears.

"Holly, take a breath and stop crying. Okay, I'll fly blind here because I really have to get back to Boston and finalize that shipping stuff with the orchids as soon as possible." Heather gave her a stern look. "Here, scroll through the microfilm. Put 'abandoned structures' in the search box and see what you can find," Heather said. "I've about had it with you, though, and the scrapes you get yourself into."

"I'm so sorry."

"Just focus and search the microfilm."

Holly searched for old Shellesby College maps and found one that looked pretty detailed. She spent five minutes studying the map, and then noticed there were three buildings that seemed very far out in the woods.

Ivy is probably in one of those, she thought.

"How are you doing? Find anything?"

"What does this mean?" Ivy showed her a little X on the map.

"I don't know. Let's look at the map legend."

They peered at the legend in the corner and found that an X meant there was a fence around the structure.

Holly noticed that of the three buildings, only one was in the proper location to see the tallest pine at the edge of the lake. But boy, that structure was exactly *above* the tallest pine at the edge of the lake, about a quarter-mile up the hill directly behind the pine.

That must be it, thought Holly.

"Okay, I'm finished. Again, I can't thank you enough. You're the best!"

She and Heather quickly left the library, and Heather turned to say goodbye.

"I'm glad you got what you needed."

"I am shattered that you're still disappointed in me."

"Well, I am."

"I promise to shape up. Please believe me. Please."

"Oh, Holly, of course." She gave her a quick hug and said, "We'll have lunch soon, and I'll want to hear that you have finally screwed your head on right, young lady!"

"I will! We will! I promise."

"Take care."

"Bye, Heather."

Holly continued again with her cloak-and-dagger hiding routine and hid her way across campus from one set of bushes to another.

She knew it. Ivy must be in that structure behind the tallest pine at the back of the lake. She knew it.

But the fence…could that fence be electrified?

Holly knew there were low stone fences and electric fences all around the campus, as they were used to keep deer out from wandering around. Was that a stone fence at the structure, or was it possibly an electric fence?

She'd have to work that detail out later. Right now, she had to deal with William, and she felt the most acute knot of tension in her stomach that she'd ever had. She felt nauseous at the thought of lying to him, but she couldn't let him in on her plan. He'd forbid it.

"I must find her. If I find her, then I will forgive myself." Holly muttered these words under her breath. "I certainly can't tell him!"

She knew he'd pin her with his laser-sharp gaze and worm

out of her every detail until he found out the whole situation. Truth was, she wasn't supposed to be at that evening dance class. She had her butt suspended, and apparently, Berkeley was right to do that, she now realized.

"I really *was* irresponsible. If I had been in my dorm last night, none of this would have happened. Ivy would have been in her dorm, too, and not a sitting duck for a kidnapper/murderer on the loose.

"And what about *William,* anyway? When he said, 'She's not the one you want,' wasn't he almost *subconsciously* tantalizing Dudley with the thought of Ivy's kidnapping? Dudley knew that Berkeley may not pay a cent for *my* safe return but would not only pay any monetary amount, but also sell his very soul for Ivy's safe return. Did William even know what he was doing, or was he so mortified at the knife at my throat that he couldn't think straight? *I can't handle this stress!*"

Holly didn't know if she could handle what she was about to do, but she had no choice.

She made her last dash from a set of bushes where she had been hiding and ran to William's cottage. Holly took out her key, slammed the door, and sank onto a sofa in the living room. She quickly rang his cell phone.

"Hi, Holls, what's up? I'm deep into transferring the golden barrel cactus into a larger pot. Unless it's important, I gotta go."

"William, this is *ultra-important.* In fact, where is the most secure place on campus we can talk?"

"Well, my Cot' is the best place. We can turn the A/C on, and that compressor makes a lot of noise outside. No one can hear us talking inside."

"Okay, I'm sorry I'm interrupting at a bad time with the cactus, but I have an absolute emergency situation that I have to talk to you about right now. Like, right this second."

William sighed. "Okay, I'm here for you, baby. I'll be there in ten minutes."

Holly paced around the room nervously, and Sweetpea picked up on her anxiety and started whining. She looked at the tiny beagle puppy and then spun away and fought back tears. *I have really messed up this time!*

Unlike the other times, this time, she was involved in a deadly, dangerous situation, and she could feel her resolve slipping. Panicking over being overheard, she ran around William's cottage and turned on every tap—the sinks in the bathroom and kitchen—then she even turned on the shower full blast. With all the water running in the house, she tried to calm herself and sank back onto his sofa to await him.

William came in the door moments later, and Sweetpea went to greet him, still whining. Reflexively, he scooped up the little dog and patted her head to calm her.

"Do I hear water running? Oh, the sink is on! How did I forget to turn that off this morning?"

Holly jumped up. "No, William, please leave that on. We need to be able to speak without being overheard. We can't risk anyone overhearing us from outside."

"Um, isn't this taking the stealthy ninja thing too far?" He wandered around his place, checking out the bathroom with its sink and shower running. "Holly! What is going on? What is so important that you are going to these ridiculous measures? Do you have classified information from the president?"

"I…I…um…I…"

"What? You are making me really nervous now. You *do* have classified information from the president of the United States?"

"Blistering bluebells, of course, I don't! Keep your voice down!"

"Keep your voice down, she yells at me…No irony there."

"Blistering bluebells, you're irritating me right now."

"Oh, you're back to the 'blistering bluebells,' huh? Do you want a few minutes to calm down, and I'll come back in an hour?"

"Well, I have a right to be mad, this could, in fact, be all *your...*" Holly immediately clapped a hand over her mouth as she almost said that it was his fault. She still hadn't fully processed whether she thought William's words of *"she's not the one you want"* were partially responsible for giving Dudley the idea to kidnap Ivy or not. She felt terrified that she almost spilled all the beans, but William didn't seem to follow her train of thought and looked like he wasn't offended.

Holly backtracked quickly. "No, William, I'm sorry!" Holly burst into tears.

"Holly, baby, come on! To the couch," William ordered her, and he led her there, and she leaned her head into his shoulder and sobbed. "It's just...I am disappointed in you."

Holly felt her whole world explode at his words. She felt demoralized beyond comprehension. The person she loved most in the world was disappointed in her. She could take Berkeley's disappointment. She could take Heather's. But she could not bear William's.

"That makes my spirit feel ground into the dirt to hear you say that."

"That wasn't my intention. I love you. I love you very much, and you're frustrating me because I know you can have a bright future around here, but you are determined to self-sabotage at every turn. It gets to me."

"You think I can have a nice future?"

"I do. Boston Botanical Garden is doing a major renovation and staff shakeup, and I hoped you might get an internship there too. But, for that, you'd need Berkeley's letter of recommendation, and I hardly need to tell you that he hates you right now."

Holly stayed silent.

"I know a way to get back into his good graces, and that's why I asked you here to talk."

William studied her. "What is it?"

"First, you said you love me. Is that correct?"

"Yes, very much."

"Okay, so if I ask you to promise me to trust me this one last time, will you totally, *totally* promise me you will listen to me first before taking action?"

"Are you in more trouble? Has something else happened?"

"Yes."

"*What?*" William exploded.

"Stop screaming!" she shouted.

"She yells at me—no irony there!"

"Well, do you promise?"

He looked at the young woman he loved and saw a frightened but determined Holly with a steely glint in her eye that made him think maybe she could even pull herself together and be the best version of Holly she could be. William decided to give her one last chance. "Okay, I promise. I'll listen to you first."

She pulled the ransom note out of her back pocket.

"Ivy's been kidnapped, and I have to find her."

"*What*? I'm calling the police!" William snatched the paper out of her hand and reached for his cell phone.

"You promised!"

"I rescind the promise, effective immediately."

"William, give me two minutes."

"Okay, two minutes." He dramatically looked at his watch on his arm. "Better start, Holly, you are actually at one minute, fifty seconds right now. Forty-five seconds…forty seconds."

"I know where she is!"

That brought his head up. "You do? Great, you can lead the police there."

"Did you see the ransom note? Dudley says he will shoot any police who approach. I can find her. I know where she is. But I have to go alone. He won't see me coming, and I have to rescue Ivy."

"How are you going to rescue her?"

"I'll need to borrow Sweetpea."

At the sound of her name, Sweetpea began to whine again. William petted her even faster.

"Sweetpea? You can't borrow her. She's *my* beagle!"

"She's half *my* beagle too!" Holly screamed in retort.

"Okay. So what do you suggest? We cut her in half like King Solomon?"

At this disturbing vision, Holly burst into tears again. "William!"

"Baby, this is going from bad to worse to worst to worstest to most worst in the whole world! This is the biggest fight in our whole relationship. We need to pull back here fast before we start saying things that will be very hard to forget."

"Here, let me read *Wikipedia*."

"I am *so* not interested in *Wikipedia* right now!"

Holly ignored him and began researching on her phone. "Here, it says bloodhounds have 230 million olfactory cells in their nose. Beagles don't have as many, but they are still amazing search and rescue SAR dogs."

"Be that as it may, Sweetpea is a puppy! She can't be expected to be a SAR dog instantly. Come on."

"I have no other choice." Holly stopped crying and looked at him with utter seriousness. "I'll only say this once. If you don't listen to me and you call the police anyway, I will leave you. It will break my heart into one million pieces, but I need to do this thing, and I need your support."

"Wow, nothing loaded there," William said. He regarded her in silence for a while. "An ultimatum, huh? Wow."

"Yes," Holly said with a depth of strength in her eyes William had never seen before.

"You just pulled the emergency brake, and now our whole relationship is on the line here about whether I listen to you in this instance?"

Holly gulped and nodded, though she couldn't meet his eyes anymore.

The atmosphere in the room positively crackled with electricity and tension. The only sounds were the rushing of water from the taps and the shower. Even Sweetpea was silent.

"Fifteen minutes ago, I was replanting the golden barrel cactus with its many thorns. But you just stabbed the biggest thorn ever into our relationship just now."

At that somber declaration, Holly snapped her eyes back to his. He looked at her steadily without smiling. Holly realized that in the two years she had known him, she had never once seen him look at her like this. Even on serious topics, he always had a kind look in his eye when he spoke to her.

At this moment, she was outside the warmth of the protective cocoon he always wrapped her in, and her heart shivered at his coldness.

He held her gaze a few more seconds, then abruptly turned and walked toward the big picture windows in his living room with Sweetpea still in his arms.

She held her breath, terrified of his next words.

"I happen to love you, *unfortunately*, so I am going to give in to your demand. I'll listen to you on this. But I am quite upset our relationship took this dark turn today. However, we'll sort that out later. Tell me what's going on."

Holly felt shaken that he mentioned trouble with their relationship and hoped she could persuade him to forgive her later.

"Okay," she gulped. "Ivy's being held in an abandoned structure deep in the woods. I believe this structure has an electrified fence, and I believe she needs me to rescue her. If we call in the police, Dudley will shoot the police and then shoot Ivy because she will no longer be useful to him. That's why I must go alone to warn her today of my rescue plan that will happen tomorrow at dawn."

"A dawn raid, huh?"

"Yes."

"Hmmm…Dudley? Wow, that psychopath is beyond belief! He just was on stage pretending to be a human being the other night during his presentation. How can he turn into some unhinged lunatic so quickly? Well, I guess we'll never fully know." William was silent a while longer, then said, "Alright. You win. Every instinct in my body is screaming at me to call the police, but I'll obey your wishes. For one day. If you don't rescue her by dawn tomorrow, I'm calling the police. I can't sit by while the director's daughter is kidnapped!"

"Thank you, William."

"So what do you want from me right now?"

"Well, to keep this a secret, I had to split the info between you and Heather. Heather knows which structure it is because she helped me with researching old maps of the college but has no idea that Ivy is probably being held there. *You* know that Ivy is kidnapped, but you don't know where the abandoned structure is."

"Why can't you trust me with it?"

"Because you'll never let me go there alone if you knew, and I can work better, faster, and undetected by myself!"

"You're right—I would never let you go there alone if I knew where it was."

"See?"

"Okay. I love you, Holly. I am trusting Ivy's life with you. I'll support you…until tomorrow.

After I give you your chance today, I'm calling the police tomorrow if you haven't found her. Deal?"

"Deal!"

"Question."

"Yes?"

"Can we turn off the faucets and shower now that we're finished with the spy stuff?"

"Yes." Holly managed a weak smile.

"Listen, baby, I stuck with you through the bats *and* the locusts *and* the flood *and* the Friar Lawrence herb tea. But I don't like being emotionally blackmailed, understand?"

"I'm sorry!"

"I come from a broken home and saw manipulative behavior all the time. I don't like it, and if it becomes a pattern, *I'll* be the one to leave *you*."

"It's only this one thing. I promise! It's…it's…it's…just…"

"Baby, it's okay. You look punished enough. You look terrified. Why don't you just let me go so I can help you?"

"I can't…"

"Okay, then you better go now and do the recon so you help poor Ivy ASAP! Take Sweetpea, but try to hold her for as long as possible so that she only has to walk when it's strictly needed. She's still so young yet."

"I will. Trust me!"

"I'll stick with you through this, Holly." With that, he pulled her into a deep kiss and fierce hug. The intensity of the last half-hour transmitted through his embrace. He was surprised at this new strength he saw in her, and it also fascinated him. He always knew she'd be a powerhouse when she got her act together.

"Gosh, I don't want to let you out that door, but you better hustle! It's already late afternoon."

"I'll let you know as soon as I'm back."

She scooped up Sweetpea and turned quickly away before her resolve left her.

"Remember, Holly, *where there's a Will, there's a way.* I

believe in you. Stay safe, get the job done, and come back immediately!"

Holly rushed out the door.

As she made her way toward the lake, she stopped briefly in the herb garden. She scanned the foliage, and once she saw what she was looking for, she knelt down and quickly picked up a few leaves.

Straightening up, she took Sweetpea's leash and led her into the Visitor Center's kitchen. She quickly put a pot on to boil the herbal leaves she'd just picked. After a few minutes, she poured the liquid into a bowl. She then went to the utility room to get an eyedropper bottle. Returning to the kitchen, she poured the liquid into the eyedropper bottle and quickly left the area before William came back from his Cot' to work again on the golden barrel cactus.

The less he knew about all her plans, the better, she thought.

She hustled to beat the sunset.

CHAPTER TWELVE

olly was jogging around the lake with Sweetpea in her arms when she heard a few mocking voices stop her.

"There she is! Ms. Poseidon herself! Goddess of the sea! Holly, we heard about the flood in the Tropical Forest Room. Don't you think you should switch majors and go into oceanography at this point?"

Nasty giggling was heard from the three girls. They were friends of Ivy's who also hated Holly.

Don't take the bait this time, Holly told herself.

"And what's that? A doggie? You know there's a no-dog rule on campus!"

Holly felt trapped.

"She's William's, and I'm taking her for a walk since I've been suspended for the day, and I have nothing else to do."

The girls giggled again. "Hopefully, that suspension turns into an outright dismissal!" They elbowed each other.

"I know, right?" one of them said.

"Nice talking to you." Holly rolled her eyes and took off running again.

Looking behind her, she saw the coast was clear. Gasping after her sprint, she put Sweetpea down and held her leash. "Give me a moment, 'Pea. Mommy needs to catch her breath." Holly took some calming breaths. "Are you proud of me? Look! First time ever that I didn't take their bait! I'm developing self-control! Who knew?"

Sweetpea wagged her tail furiously and gave three short barks.

"A three-bark salute, huh? I'll take it!" Holly beamed at her little dog.

Glancing anxiously at the sun lowering in the sky, she judged she only had about forty-five minutes of light left.

"Sweetpea, let's get this in gear!"

She jogged to the part of the lake that seemed directly below where the abandoned structure might be. She stopped just short of the tallest pine because she didn't want to step right into view of where Dudley might be monitoring.

She pulled Ivy's gardening apron she'd snatched off a hook in the greenhouse a few minutes ago out of her backpack. Holly let Sweetpea sniff it to get Ivy's scent in her little nostrils. "Come on, baby, we need you. Ivy needs you."

The little dog sniffed the apron, then turned and made a beeline ten feet back from where they already came.

"Are you sure, baby? Do you think it's here? The map seemed to put it farther north." Holly wrinkled her brow as she thought. "Okay, well, maybe Dudley cut across that way on his way to the structure. I'll trust you. You have 230 million more olfactory cells in your nose than me. You're the expert."

The little dog now determinedly tugged on the leash and led Holly off the path at the lake and deep into the forest and up the hill.

"I'm going to even take my shoes off," Holly said. "That way I can walk even more quietly." Wincing at the stones that occasionally littered the forest floor, Holly let Sweetpea pull her steadily upward.

The puppy led Holly up past the last of the trees, and suddenly, the sight of the abandoned building came into view. It had a tall electric fence around it, and a large tree was in the southwest corner of the yard. It was a sugar maple tree, and one of its branches hung out far outside over the fence.

Holly involuntarily gasped.

She saw Ivy kneeling down and picking dandelion leaves.

Her hair was matted, and when she stood up to move to a different patch of grass, Holly noticed she had a pronounced limp. The sun caught her full in the face, and it looked like she had a black eye and other bruising.

At the sound of Holly's gasp, Ivy froze. She looked up with a stricken look in her eye, like a deer in headlights. Ivy looked right and left to try to identify where the sound had come from.

Holly gasped again.

This time, Ivy identified the location of the sound, and suddenly, her shocked ice-blue eyes locked with Holly's shocked green ones.

Now, it was Ivy's turn to gasp.

"Shhhh," Holly said. "Are you okay?"

"No, I'm hurt."

"Shhhh, quiet! Don't even look at me. Talk in a whisper. Where is he?"

Ivy jerked a thumb over her shoulder. "In the backyard."

"Okay, don't look at me when you talk and make sure you're almost not audible."

Ivy stared at her.

"Remember? I'm your new life coach. You must listen to me and do exactly as I tell you. Your life is in danger."

"I know it is!"

"So, listen. *I'm going to rescue you, I swear it,* but not today. I'm coming back for you tomorrow."

"Tomorrow?"

"If I told the police about you now, they'd come up here, stampeding with all their K-9 units and rescue helicopters. Dudley would hear them a mile away. I know that he has a gun and wants to shoot any police that might come along with ransom money."

"Exactly!"

"So, we have to do this together. Listen to me. Catch this."

Holly threw over the fence the eyedropper filled with liquid.

"Go find it."

Ivy went to pick it up and then quickly hid it in her jeans pocket. "Okay, what is it?"

"It's cayenne pepper liquid. By the way, I guess the fence is electrified?"

"Yes, he knows where to turn it off, but he makes sure I'm not with him, so I don't know how."

"Okay, so listen. By the way, is there a clock in there?"

"No."

"We'll have to use Mother Nature's alarm clock: the sunrise. Tomorrow at first light, you're going to surprise him in his sleep. You'll take this eyedropper bottle and drop this liquid onto his eyes. He'll awaken, and that's when you drop another drop or two in his open eyes, and then you run."

"That's very dangerous!"

"You bet it is! You'll be in total mortal danger at that point. He'll be as mad as a bear and come after you. You can't doubt yourself or me. You must execute this plan we're hatching to the letter."

"That *you* are hatching."

"Yes, that I am hatching. Listen up! After the eyedropper stuff, run. *Run! Run!* He'll get his gun and come for you. You need to run out the door and climb that tree and jump off the branch that hangs over the fence."

"*What?* I'm severely injured! He dragged me up here, and I tripped over a fallen log, and he didn't stop but just dragged me over it, so my leg is really bad. I can't climb!"

"You have to!"

"I can't!"

"Life is not a dress rehearsal. This is your only option. Meanwhile, I'll be up here exactly at dawn tomorrow. I'll give a signal, and the police forces from eight towns and a rescue helicopter will be here in a moment as a backup."

"They will?"

"Yes, but we need you over the fence before they come!"

"*I can't climb!*"

"You'll have to. Tomorrow will be the most difficult day of your life. Once you squirt the liquid from the eyedropper into his eyes, you're starting a chain of dominos that will not end until you are either rescued, or he shoots you. I'm here to make sure you're rescued."

"Holly, I'm scared. No, I'm terrified."

"You should be. That means all your instincts will be on high alert, and your survival sense will help you get through it. Don't think of the pain in your leg. See that low branch on your side?"

"Yes."

"You need to get up onto that and then swing up to the next branch."

"Oh my gosh."

"Then, lie down on that branch and, while hugging the branch with your legs, crawl on that branch inch by inch over the fence and, when you are cleared of the fence, jump down into the grass here on my side. Hug the branch like a koala bear!"

"Oh. My. Gosh."

"Take a good long look at the tree now and until he takes you back inside. Don't let him catch you looking at the tree, though! Memorize the steps: Dawn, eyedropper, run, first branch, swing up to the second branch, hug the tree and koala across over the fence, jump off."

"Koala across?"

"Yes, a new verb I just made up. To 'koala' means hug the tree with your arms and legs and scoot across the branch to safety!"

"I have no words."

"By then, the police will join us up here. So, help is on the way, but you need to get over that fence by yourself first."

"How will they know to come here?"

"I'll give them a signal."

"What kind of signal?"

"You'll see tomorrow. I'll be here. I promise. I have to go now before it gets too dark for me to see my way back down."

With that, Holly turned and put Sweetpea down to have her lead them back to the lake. Rocks hurt her bare feet, and she had to keep brushing branches out of the way as the little dog sped down the hill, retracing the steps they'd climbed earlier.

Finally emerging onto the lake path again, Holly put her running shoes back on and scooped the puppy into her arms. She jogged quickly off campus and back up the path to William's house, breathing heavily.

"William, it's me. Open up, please."

She only had time to knock once before he tore open the door.

"Well, how did it go? Is she there?"

"No. No. No, I can't believe it. She wasn't there!" Holly said with a wild-eyed look. She had debated with herself all the way back whether she should tell William that she'd found Ivy.

Holly remembered that he might still be nursing wounded

pride because of her demand earlier. He was a master chess player and could checkmate her with a reciprocal demand. Demanding that she tell him where she is, or *he* would leave *her*.

If William decided to play hardball and give her a taste of her own medicine, what bitter medicine that would be. In a toss-up between keeping her relationship with him and protecting Ivy, she would choose William any day. But, if he forced her to tell him where Ivy was and he decided to call the police anyway, Dudley might shoot Ivy if he felt cornered by the cops.

She didn't know if he would understand Ivy was in real danger if Dudley saw the police coming. Holly thought it was safer for her to rescue Ivy tomorrow by herself, remaining undetected in the forest as she approached, and then she felt she could coach Ivy through the rescue itself. To protect Ivy and her relationship with him, she decided lying was her best choice.

"No, she wasn't there. I don't know what to do!"

She handed Sweetpea back to him. "This little girl did her best, but we came up empty-handed."

"Well, there's nothing we can do at the moment. It's past sunset now and getting darker by the minute. I'll call the police at first light. We want the police to be able to be stealthy in their rescue. Dudley said in his note that he's watching the place and will shoot her if he sees police approach. If we go now at night, he'll see the police lights from far away. They'd have to use flashlights to search in this darkness. So, come in, baby. Take a shower—that is if we have any water left— and I'll give you a shoulder massage. Your shoulders are tensed all the way up to your ears from all this stress."

"I'd love to, but Berkeley has suspended me, and I'm supposed to stay inside my dorm. If he found out I'm here tonight, he might throw me out for good. I'd better be in for bed check if it comes to that."

"Yes, good idea."

Holly only ducked out because she could not possibly keep up the ruse for a whole night. William read her like a book because she could never hide her feelings from him. She had an extremely difficult time lying for even two minutes, let alone for the next twelve hours! Better to let him think she had failed. She felt relieved he seemed to understand they had to be stealthy in the rescue attempt, but she still felt the burden of guilt overwhelming her. Holly felt that had she never taken Ivy to that evening dance class, then Ivy would still be safe and sound.

She may have just failed her chemistry and world history tests, but she was *not* going to fail this life test. If she ever wanted to look herself in the eye in the mirror again, Holly knew she needed to rescue Ivy herself.

"I'd better go now."

"Holly, I love you. See you tomorrow. We'll get Ivy. Don't worry."

"Okay, goodnight," she said, reaching up for her goodbye kiss.

"Bye, baby."

Holly turned and headed for her dorm. Exhausted by the day, she was still so wound up; she felt that she might not get any sleep at all.

CHAPTER THIRTEEN

*H*olly had been up all night, but when she saw the clock say 5:00 a.m., she got up out of bed. She silently put clothes on, and then she let herself out of her room and exited her dorm. Making a beeline to the Science Center, she climbed the fire escape ladder up to the roof. Since she was suspended, her ID swipe card was deactivated at the moment, and she couldn't get into the Science Center properly. But the fire escape stairs were still open to her.

Where there's a Holly, there's a way, she thought. *I've got to tell William my new jingle!*

"Hi, Snapdragon," Holly crooned to the beautiful pigeon.

She looked around and got the smallest carrier on the shelf next to his coop. "Hey, boy, you're going to be the big hero of the day today! Come, let's rescue Ivy!" She coaxed the bird into the carrier and closed his coop door.

Holly ran down the fire escape ladder and jumped off. She jogged for about five minutes to the west where William's Cot' was.

She knocked on his door and held her breath. "William! I need you now! Please come to the door."

189

William opened the door a couple of minutes later, wearing only his boxers.

"Holly! What's wrong?" He took in her frightened eyes and pinched look and saw her holding Snapdragon's carrier.

"What is that? What are you doing with Snapdragon at this hour?"

"No time. I'm rescuing Ivy right this second. I have no time to explain."

"What? You said you didn't see her yesterday!"

"Well, um...that was not the truth."

"Holly!"

"No time! I'm leaving right this second. I only came to tell you so you can alert the police. Please mobilize every K-9 unit in the surrounding eight towns and tell them we need the rescue helicopter too!"

"I will! But what has Snapdragon got to do with it?"

"I'll deploy him right where Ivy is being held! He'll circle around a bit, and then his homing instincts will lead him back here. So, where you see him in the air, run toward that part of the forest. We'll be a quarter-mile up the hill at an abandoned structure."

"What?"

"Um...I also need to borrow Sweetpea so I can find that structure again," Holly said meekly.

"What?"

"No time! Please get Sweetpea on a leash. I've got to go. If I don't, Ivy will die. Trust me. I saw Dudley, and he looks like a psychopath now!"

"After this is finished, you're going to get a stern lecture!"

"I can't wait. I've gotta go now, though."

"Holly..."

"I'm going!" She grabbed Sweetpea's leash out of his hand and turned to go. "Please rescue us with the police. We'll need them."

"Holly…"

And she turned to look at him once more. "I love you."

"I love you too."

As Holly turned to leave, she heard William dialing 911.

Holly ran soundlessly around the lake with the last of the moonlight. When she got to the part of the lake where the trail to Ivy branched off, she saw that dawn was just starting to break. The barest hint of light allowed the forest to come into focus, and she plowed ahead with Sweetpea. She put the little dog down and let her sniff Ivy's gardening apron again to give her back the scent.

The little dog took off into the forest, and Holly ran behind while clutching Snapdragon's carrier.

She finally emerged from the forest and saw the abandoned structure again. Holly saw a little outcropping of rocks with a scrub bush nearby. She tied Sweetpea's leash to the scrub brush, and now, the little dog was hidden from view by the rocks.

"Shhhh, Sweetpea. I'll come back for you. Or Ivy will. Or William will. Or the police will. You must stay here, darling, so you're out of sight."

She turned and looked at the structure.

Ivy's terrified face looked out at her from a window.

She's been waiting for me, Holly thought.

She straightened up and opened Snapdragon's carrier. The magnificently colored pigeon zoomed in circles for a bit, and then ascended to the treetops. After one final circle, Snapdragon turned south and made a beeline to his coop back at the Science Center roof.

Ivy stared at her with her mouth open, and Holly gave her a thumbs up. Ivy immediately turned away from the window and went into the back of the room.

Holly pulled out her cell phone and rang William. "Do you see Snapdragon deployed?"

"Got 'em," William said, squinting into his binoculars. "There are fourteen pairs of K-9 dogs and cops ringing the lake here. They see where Snapdragon is flying from, and they know where you are now. They'll be there in a few minutes."

His voice was getting drowned out by the *whomp-whomp-whomp* of the rescue helicopter flying over him.

"The chopper is coming too! That will be there first!"

"Great, because I think—" and she was cut off by the most ungodly scream she'd ever heard. "Dudley is awake, and the dominos are falling!" Holly screamed.

"What? What dominos?" William asked.

"Never mind that. Just come get us!" Holly waited just long enough for him to assure her he was coming and then ended the call.

Holly pocketed her phone right when Dudley burst through the door, holding his eyes and cursing as viciously as he knew how.

"I'm going to kill you, you horrendous girl!"

Ivy ran out the door in a flash and made a beeline for the tree. She was visibly limping but running as though her life depended on it. She fell in the meadow as she ran toward the tree but picked herself up and kept going.

"Ivy, I'm here! I'll keep him off—keep going!"

Ivy found another gear and got up the first branch of the tree. "I'm over here, Dudley!" Holly screamed.

Dudley paused and then viciously pawed at his eyes to try to see. He ran around in a zig-zag pattern to figure out where her voice came from. "Where are you, you stupid girl?"

"I'm over here!"

"There?"

"I'm here! Come and get me, you psycho!"

"Holly, I can't swing up to that other branch!"

"You have to!"

Dudley started shooting.

"Ivy, hurry!"

"I can't!"

"Holly? You're here too? I'll kill both of you!" Dudley threw his gun on the ground and went to his garden hose. Turning it on, he poured the water onto his face to stop the stinging from the cayenne pepper. With a few more grunts of pain, he tossed the hose aside and wiped his eyes.

He picked up his gun and shot at Ivy again.

"Help me, Holly!" Ivy screamed.

"Koala across!"

Holly tried to hide behind the rock outcropping and poked her head over it to get a read on the situation.

Dudley suddenly turned to the back of the house and went to a box on the structure's wall. He turned off the electricity on the fence and came roaring forward. "I'll get you both!"

Ivy screamed and jumped down from her branch.

"I made it! I made it!"

Holly untied Sweetpea's leash and ran toward Ivy.

Dudley started to shoot at them with a *pop-pop-pop* sound.

Suddenly, they heard the *whomp-whomp* of the rescue helicopter as it came into view. The door opened, and a sniper looked down at them with his gun in ready position.

"Run!" Holly said.

She and Ivy ran down the hill, but Dudley's bullets rained down in their vicinity and bounced off the trees.

"Duck," Holly said, and she held a large branch from one of the trees out of the way while they ran away from the structure.

One of Dudley's bullets caught Holly in the calf, and she screamed in pain.

"Arghh, Ivy, I'm hit!"

Ivy screamed in terror, and Holly dropped Sweetpea's leash. The little beagle barked madly and ran around Holly.

Right then, the sniper in the chopper shot Dudley in the leg, and he went down.

"You jerks, you'll never take me alive!"

He shot his gun at himself, but he had run out of bullets.

Right then, the K-9 dogs and cops came into the clearing and surrounded them. They arrested Dudley.

William was right behind them and immediately scooped up Holly and ran toward the rescue helicopter that landed on the grass near the structure. "She's shot! She needs medical attention ASAP!" He looked at her. "Are you okay? When I heard you scream, I felt like I had been shot!"

"William," Holly's voice sounded soft because she was in shock from the turn of the events.

"William, I have something I want to say to you."

"Yes! What is it?"

"William, I have a little...what's it called...a jingle I made up."

"Okay..."

"Wait for it, ready? *Where there's a Holly, there's a way!* How about that? Like it?"

William looked at her with tears in his eyes, and he couldn't speak. He tightened his grip on her and pressed the most loving kiss to her forehead. "It's perfect. My heart is so full I can hardly talk. You are the bravest and most ingenious person I ever met. You are my everything." He hugged her tight. "You're also in big trouble with me, young lady, for putting yourself in such terrible danger...but you're a genius! The bravest genius I know."

He deposited her in the rescue helicopter.

"It kills me to leave you, but I have to settle poor Ivy. She's in bad shape, too, and Berkeley. Oh my God, Berkeley! He'll go nuclear on everyone and everything when he gets wind of this, but I'll make sure he knows that the real heroine today was Holly Jackson. I'll see you ASAP after I take care of every-thing." He glanced at her. "Baby, you *are* my everything."

"Same," Holly said with her heart in her eyes.

CHAPTER FOURTEEN

*H*olly had moved altogether into William's Cot' after they had released her from the hospital. Luckily, the bullet only grazed her calf, and it was healing nicely now.

She hadn't been back to class since then because Berkeley was so utterly grateful to her that he ordered her professors to give her an A+ in all her classes for that semester so she could focus on studying for her internship at the Boston Botanical Garden.

His letter of recommendation was so glowing that they were also considering fast-tracking her to a permanent position.

William showered her with affection and flowers. He brought in plant after flowering plant from the greenhouse into his Cot' to brighten Holly's spirits.

The most amazing tropical flowers overflowed in every room of his place, and he also bought out the entire store of get-well-soon balloons.

Holly sat on the sofa, cuddling Sweetpea and studying the Latin names of the Boston Garden's fern collection, since she was going to be in charge of that collection right away. She saw Ivy coming up through the big picture window and went to greet her.

"Come in! How are you feeling?"

"I'm okay. My leg is still bothering me a bit, but it'll be alright. I brought you some of these amazing wildflowers I found over by my dorm. What are these?"

"Those are wild asters—very pretty. Thank you! Here, I'll put them in a vase on the dining room table. Stay for dinner! I went into the vegetable garden and picked anything ripe I could find and threw it in a pot. It'll be yummy."

"Your food is always yummy. You're a great cook. Listen, Holly, I can't even begin…"

"It's not necessary. It's okay!"

"I'm an only child, but you are my legit sister!"

"I'm also so…"

"Not necessary. It's okay."

Ivy gave her a quick embrace.

"Oh, there's William. I see him walking up. I better go."

"No, stay for dinner!"

"No, I'm going, but I'll be by tomorrow for leftovers for lunch. How about that?"

She got up and walked out the door William held open for her.

"Hi, William. Bye, William. Bye, Holly."

"Your lunch reservation is confirmed! See ya!"

Holly noticed Ivy had stopped flirting with William, and that made her much happier overall.

"Ivy looks better. How is she feeling?"

"She's good. Still a little problem with her leg, but she says she's improving."

"I heard from Berkeley that Dudley will stay the rest of his life behind bars for the kidnapping and also the murder of Ogletree."

"Well, that only seems right, I imagine," Holly agreed. "I've also told the police what I overheard Dudley say in the greenhouse about Ogletree killing those two students, so at least we know all the mysteries are solved now."

William headed to the kitchen and went over to the stove. "What is that heavenly smell?"

"It's my world-famous ratatouille!"

"I saw you from the Science Center lounge's window. You combed through the veggie garden extensively today."

"Well, they're all in here now." She lifted the lid of the pot and took a spoon out and gave him a taste of her seasoned vegetables.

"You need to open a restaurant, baby. This is scrumptious."

"Well, the restaurant can wait. I have my internship to do first."

"I am so proud of you. I have no words. When I get back tonight, I'll help you study and will quiz you on your ferns."

"William, you won't believe this. Berkeley has me scheduled for a portrait sitting tomorrow in the Camellia Room."

"Wow, really?"

"Yes!"

"Well, he told me he considers you an honorary Berkeley daughter now, so you know that the portrait has to happen at this point. I don't know how you are going to sit still with your mouth closed for that long." William slapped his thigh in mirth. "I'll have to peek in at these portrait sessions. I think he'd be better off just taking a photo of you and blowing it up to portrait size. It would be kinder on you."

"Maybe that can happen." Holly laughed.

"Baby, come over to the greenhouse at 7:00 p.m. after dinner. I'm working late but come by then. I have a surprise for you."

"Can't you just bring the flowering pot over here like all the others?"

"Um, no, this one is a bit different. Plus, I'm sure you'd like to see the greenhouse again after two weeks."

"Well, that's true. Okay, I'll be over there!"

William bent down to kiss her and left. "Seven p.m., right after sunset!"

As she watched William go, she felt such pride in herself. She had managed to stop shooting herself in the foot and had gotten out of her own way, and now she was unstoppable.

Holly went out to sit on his stoop to watch the sunset. She became lost in thought as she dreamed about becoming as accomplished a botanist as he was. He would love it if she could talk botany on his level.

Maybe I can also make discoveries someday and be featured in Horticultural Digest *myself. Wouldn't that be a hoot!*

Shaking herself from her daydreaming, she realized the day had turned to night and went in to change her top.

She was excited he had some sort of surprise lined up for her, so she changed into her pretty peasant blouse he had complimented her on many times before. Holly applied a little lipstick and blush, and then leaned over the dining room table and picked the top of one of Ivy's asters she had brought her and tucked the flower behind her ear. Her luxurious red cloud of curls softly framed her face.

She dabbed on a little mascara and laughed. "I'm not even scared of makeup anymore!" Holly gave her reflection a wink and then headed out the door.

Holly took a look at Sweetpea to see if she should bring her, but the little dog was so happily gnawing on one of her toy bones that she decided not to disturb her. The small beagle puppy made chewing sounds amid little growls of happiness.

She pulled the door closed and walked over to the greenhouse. Holly walked toward the Visitors' Center door.

"Holly, is that you? Good." William came out. "Shh, here, let me lead you in. It's a surprise. Close your eyes."

"I hate surprises! Even when I was a kid!"

"Shh, just come. No peeking!" He led her inside. "Okay. Here, wait right here."

"What, what, what is going on?"

"Can you close your eyes and *also* your mouth? Maybe for just one second?"

"William!" Holly laughed. She felt him lead her through the Visitors' Center meeting room and turn her right as they entered the Desert Room.

"What? Did you bring me here to see the golden barrel cactus? Really?"

"Um, no, it's not the golden barrel cactus. Okay, you can open now."

Holly opened her eyes and gasped. She saw the one lone cereus blossom open, and it looked perfect.

"How, how…?"

"Well, this bud hadn't opened, and if I left it alone, it would have grown hard and withered up. I injected it every day with a fertilizer with very high sugar content, and I got it to open for you."

Holly cried. She was so touched.

"Do you like it? I think it's exquisite."

Holly admired the one lone blossom. Eight inches across, it was the purest white with little yellow highlights among the edges of the petal. The most beautiful scent filled the room, and the petals looked like they were made from the finest soft silk.

She felt beyond touched he had done this for her.

Changing the mood, William joked, "I've heard that night-blooming cereus are in the mistletoe family, and you know how you have to kiss under a mistletoe!" He led her directly under the flower.

"Will-iam! That is so horse chestnuts! They are most certainly *not* in the mistletoe family!"

"Frankly, my dear, I don't care!" And with that, he ushered her into a laid-back swoon and gave her a deep, loving kiss.

She giggled when he set her upright again.

"You are the true queen of the night! You went from high to low and from low to *grow*! You grew into the best version of Holly you can be! I'm so proud of you, baby, I can't stand it…If only you wouldn't put the rest of us through such stress with your…um…growing pains…but it's all good."

Holly cried. "Are you proud of me?" Holly said tremulously.

"I'll burst if I have any more pride for you." He beamed down at her for another moment. "Hey, this is a bloom party! How's your calf?"

"It feels okay."

"Up to a little dancing?"

"Sure!"

William got his cell phone out and put some gentle music on. He took her in his arms for some slow dancing.

Holly leaned into him and smelled his aftershave. "What did you use?" Holly asked as she gently leaned back in and nuzzled his cheek for a good whiff of a delicious pine smell she thought she identified.

"It's called Divine Pine. I thought you'd like it."

"Love it. Buy it again!" She leaned her cheek onto his chest and put her right hand over his heart—the heart he said he loved her with. She had found someone who could handle her swirling deep emotions and provide her with the steadiness she craved. Life felt perfect right now, and she wished she could bottle up this moment to cherish forever.

"Here, come with me, baby." William led her through the exit door, then through the Camellia Room and into the Tropical Forest Room. He switched the music to something with a faster tempo and asked, "How's the leg?"

"It's fine!"

"This is called the 'Waltz of the Flowers' from Tchaikovsky's *The Nutcracker!*'"

"I know this. I used to dance ballet in high school."

Laughing, they smashed together into a facsimile of a ball-room dance hold, their chins lifted and heads held pretentiously high.

"Dance!" he commanded.

As Tchaikovsky's music roared and soared, they whirled and twirled, tangled and tangoed, bumbled and stumbled, and laughed their way around and amongst the hundreds of flowers and trees in the darkened and empty greenhouse.

"We're making a blooming mess!" Holly yelled over the music. Dozens of flowers had been knocked off their branches as they stampeded around the plants and bushes.

"Well, it's a bloom party, right? I'll rake everything up in the morning. Let go, baby. Enjoy yourself."

William looked ultra-attractive with a flush to his cheeks. The blush Holly had put on earlier was far eclipsed by her rosy cheeks, giving her the most perfect peaches-and-cream complexion. Her eyes sparkled with the most amazing, mischievous glow. William thought she had never looked so beautiful. He impulsively picked her up by her waist and twirled her around and around again, which made her peasant blouse fly out around her. Then he gently put her down and stared at her intently.

"Come with me back to the Desert Room, baby. I have one last surprise for you."

"You do?"

"I do."

He led her back to the Desert Room and settled her on a chair he had brought in. "Can you possibly close your eyes again, or is that pushing my luck?"

"For you, I'll close my eyes…just this once. Don't get used to it."

"I wouldn't dream of it, little prickly pear." He left her for a few minutes.

"William, I'm wait-ing!"

'Coming! Coming! Eyes closed!"

Holly heard rustling. She heard him grunt once when he put something obviously heavy onto the floor.

"What's going on here?"

"Open sesame!"

Holly opened her eyes in time to see William lift up the lid of a fish tank. This tank had no water in it, but thousands of little fireflies.

"This is your proper Night Lights Ball, Holly, and you are the legit queen of the night!"

As he lifted the lid, thousands of tiny fireflies flew out of the tank and filled the Desert Room with tiny pinpoints of light.

Holly was enchanted and reached out a palm to let a firefly touch it.

"I'm speechless. What's this?"

"I grew them in the Science Center with our grow lights. I wanted a very special memorable night for you. One that you'll never forget. This is to celebrate you. All your bravery, genius, and okay…even your drama." William laughed.

He watched as she got up from the chair and spun around gently, looking at the magical fireflies filling the room.

"I feel like this is a magical moment. Thank you for this precious night."

She went to kiss him, and he held her tight in his embrace.

"Here, we must open the retractable roof to let them fly away, lest I have to sweep up thousands of little fireflies tomorrow."

"Not the roof! Be 'cereus,' William! The bats will come for the cereus, and then I'll be back to literal square one!"

"Relax, baby, I'm way ahead of you. I'll stand by the emergency door and look out. At the first sign of bats, I'll close the roof."

"I should have known. Where there's a Will, there's a way."

"Well, where there's a Holly, there's also a way."

Holly felt her heart would burst with happiness. She gave him a thousand-firefly-watt smile.

"Here we go! Roof opening in three...two...one." He pressed the button, and the retractable roof slid open.

The fireflies streamed out, and soon, the very last ones had floated into the night.

"I see the Milky Way stars," Holly breathed.

"Me, too, but let's get that roof closed before the bats come!"

"Agreed!" Holly said.

He pushed the button, and the roof slid closed.

"So," William said.

"So," Holly said.

"Like it?"

"I *loved* it."

"Let's go back home. I'm starving. I want nothing more than a huge plate of your ratatouille and then to pet Sweetpea on the couch while I quiz you on your ferns."

"Let's go," Holly said with her heart in her eyes.

He looped an arm around her, and they walked toward the exit.

Suddenly, her face lit up with an evil grin.

Ye Gods, why have I not thought of this before? Holly asked herself.

Unerringly, her hand found his ribs, and she started tickling him.

William jumped in surprise. "What, what's this? Hahaha, oh, Holly, *stop*. I am very ticklish!"

Holly's evil grin deepened as she kept up her devastatingly accurate gentle assault on his ribs.

"Holly, *please*, I beg you, *stop*. That's my weakness. It's my Achilles' heel!"

"Well, Achilles, it's about time we started discovering *your* weaknesses. We have been discussing *mine* for days now." Holly laughed, absolutely delighted with herself.

William roared with laughter, both from her comments and from her unerring hands doing their best to tickle him into the next century.

"Wow! Is this the 'new' Holly? The *'large and in-charge'* version? Consider me fascinated. I can't wait to see what this next year will be like with you now that you have hit your stride."

Holly was delighted by his words.

"Alright. I'll take pity on you. I'll keep *my* hands quiet if you keep *your* hands quiet. I declare a 'tickle-free zone'," Holly said as she stopped tickling him and snaked a hand gently around his waist.

"Oh boy, she drives a hard bargain! Mercenary little prickly pear if I ever did see one!"

William couldn't stop laughing.

"You're priceless, Holly. I'll never get enough of you!"

"Well, 'mission accomplished' then," Holly said. "That was my goal with you all along."

He leaned down and gave the top of her head a kiss.

"Come, baby, let's go home."

She looked up at him and gave him her most loving smile.

She then turned forward again and leaned into him as they went out the door and walked home to their future.

INTERESTED IN A FREE BOOK
FROM KIRA SEAMON?

Keep up to date with the latest news, upcoming releases, and free books from Author Kira Seamon by visiting her website.

https://www.kiraseamonauthor.com

WORD FROM THE AUTHOR

I would like to thank master horticulturalist David Sommers of Wellesley College, without whom this book would never have happened.

I also would like to thank my Fairy Bookmother, *the Jedi Master of Editing*, without whom this book also would never have happened.

I would also like to thank my other editors and beta-reader team. You all helped improve the book, thank you!

A little about me. I was born in Honolulu, Hawaii. I had a magical childhood overflowing with botany. My home had one of the best private Japanese gardens on the island of Oahu! My parents created all the details of the garden themselves, despite having no initial idea of gardening, both having lived in apartments growing up. They painstakingly created the cobblestone pathways around the "islands" they created in the backyard.

Each island had traditionally shaped Japanese plants, like pine and ironwood trees. They also incorporated many tropical plants into the scheme, though they were all very heavily pruned to keep the resemblance of a Japanese garden. My garden had fruit trees, surinam cherry, star fruit, and guava. They created in-ground koi ponds, replete with koi, goldfish, and lily pads. We had bunnies in hutches, we kept birds, we had a cat, and I had my very own hound dog, Sarah, a basset hound. We had turtles, both aquatic and land turtles. I loved walking into the garden to try to find the turtles. Sometimes I did; sometimes I couldn't find them.

We had a huge eucalyptus tree called a "silver dollar tree," which had silvery leaves that glinted in the sun. My mom told me that when I was a baby, she put me down in my playpen that was parked right next to the window in the living room that looked out on the eucalyptus tree. She said I used to be fascinated by the leaves blowing in the gentle Hawaiian breeze and could watch them quietly for an hour. Later as a preteen and teenager, I had a rope attached to that eucalyptus tree, and I would take a book with me and climb to the high branches. These were up so high, they were even with the roof! In fact, I transferred once to the roof, just for fun, though my parents weren't likewise amused! I was proud of my calluses and spent any free time I had up there reading.

We grew herbs. We grew aloe and had a huge Mexican oregano bush. I have many fond memories of me as a tiny girl given the direction by my mom to go out in the yard and break off a few sprigs of oregano to put into whatever dish she was cooking. To this day, the smell of oregano in tomato sauce transports me instantly back to my childhood.

My dad fell in love with the art of bonsai, and we had easily over a hundred bonsai on the tables behind our house. I remember him sitting at our outdoor table in the side yard with intense concentration as he poured over an open bonsai book, then tried to prune the tiny trees he had arranged in front of him.

We also were orchid fanatics. We would tear ourselves away from our garden on the weekends to travel to every corner of the island for the orchid shows that were held every Saturday. I remember munching on a star fruit from our garden, the juice dripping down my chin as I wandered around the place counting our orchids. They were growing as nature intended them; my Dad had tied them into our trees, and now they provided a gorgeous tropical look to enhance the garden's effect. I lost track after counting at least a hundred in our trees. Big ones, small ones, rare ones. The prize orchid was our dangling yellow chain orchid. They went through their natural life cycles, so some were dormant, while others were blooming.

In addition to orchid shows, my Dad took me every weekend to Foster Gardens, which is Honolulu's Botanical Gardens. It has its very own corpse flower! I grew up playing at the Foster Gardens and seeing gigantic sago palms that made me think a dinosaur must be lurking nearby.

I remember him taking me regularly to a playground a little farther away than usual that had wild cherry tomatoes along the outer edge of the grounds. I remember popping those in my mouth and thinking how fun plants were.

Inspired by all this, I once tried to pick all our flowers, and I put them in a bucket with water and swished the whole mass around. I was dismayed with my result! I was trying to create a perfume, but my mom had to gently tell me that they use only the essence of flowers for perfume-making; something that totally escaped my eight-year-old comprehension.

I also went to the prestigious Punahou School, which is known for its night-blooming cereus plant hedge! This 300-meter hedge grows along the lava rock wall that encircles the campus. It is believed that their hedge was grown from the very first cutting that was introduced to the Hawaiian Islands in 1836. In fact, it is also believed that most of the entire island of Oahu's night-blooming cereus plants were originated from cuttings from Punahou's wall!

So, when I moved to Boston, I eventually started to miss all the greenery and flowers during the harsh New England winters. This became especially pronounced in the winter of 2017. I had heard about the Wellesley College greenhouses from a friend and thought this might be a great time to check them out. I was enchanted when I stepped through their doors because here were the flowers of my youth growing heartily despite the bitter cold outside!

I found myself going there every day; it became the highlight of my day. I talked to master horticulturalist David Sommers, and he showed me the different Latin names of the plants and what they were commonly called. I took my dad with me every day, and he would fall asleep on the bench in what I called the "Tropical Forest Room" in the book. This bench was tucked away off the path, literally sitting amidst the tall Guadalupe palm and the giant white bird of paradise plant. The bench had very comfy cushions, and Dad would fall asleep beside me. Even though David and other staff were around, the place was often deserted, and sometimes I didn't see another soul for the entire duration of my visit.

I remember thinking one day, *This place would be a good setting for a mystery book—it's so mysterious.* About ten minutes later, with my dad snoring beside me all the while, the thought came to me: *Do I need to be the one to write that mystery book about the greenhouses?*

Well, once the thought took root, (pardon the botanical pun), there was no going back. There was a young student working in the greenhouses who had red hair, so she became my inspiration for Holly. The greenhouses were just getting ready for their annual light show, which became a huge blowout event in my book. Wellesley's Annual Light Show was a considerably smaller affair, but it was absolutely magical to walk in the greenhouses at night with the special lights on.

Alas, the Wellesley College Greenhouses in that iteration

are no more. I heard that they found lead in the paint, and there were other structural issues cropping up. It was scheduled for demolition. As luck would have it, right before it was scheduled to be razed, their prize Queen of the Night night-blooming cereus plant was set to bloom! David invited me to their bloom party, and it was a true highlight of all my experiences there at the greenhouses.

I remember walking around the lake quietly in the moonlight while waiting until it was the right time to start the party. I was so bubbling over with excitement I couldn't stand it! Finally, I walked over to the greenhouses and noticed I was the first one to arrive. I walked around and around in the empty parking lot until David drove up. He opened the greenhouses, and from the first moment I set foot inside, I was greeted by the most beautiful scent ever! Literally bouncing off the walls now with excitement, I ran down the hallway and turned left into the room where the cereus was. I yelped in pleasure when I saw them for the first time. In all my years at Punahou, I had never actually seen the blooms. They open only at night, and I didn't live close to the school, so I was never at that part of the island at night. So, this was my first experience with the blossoms. They really do open rather quickly, almost like watching a time-lapse film in real- time. They are of the softest silken feel, and they look breathtaking. I left around 10:00 p.m., and David said that by the morning, they had totally wilted. I took photos of them, but I also purchased exquisite photos David took during his many years at the college. These are on my www.deadcereus.com website.

So, in conclusion, gentle reader, it would be my hope that you might be inspired to bring a little more "plant power" into your life!

Get you to a farmer's market.

Try a new vegetable.

Try a few new vegetables!

Then throw them in a pot and make Holly's World-Famous Ratatouille, a recipe is included at the back of the book.

Go to a nursery. Ask questions of the staff; they'll be happy to help.

Grow some herbs!

Or at least pick up some fresh ones in the produce section of your supermarket.

Dunk a sprig of fresh lavender into your tea.

How about fresh mint?

The worlds of plants, botany, and horticulture are fascinating places, and if my book has inspired you and I brought you one step closer to enjoying any of them, then my mission will have been completed. For your enjoyment, I'm including recipes for some of the sumptuous dishes described herein. Enjoy! *Bon Appetit*!

ABOUT THE AUTHOR

Kira Kanani Seamon was born and raised in Hawaii. A polymath, Kira is a gold medal/state winner in piano performance and a National and two-time Regional Dance Champion. She's an award-winning photographer and has had her art accepted and sold in national and regional juried shows. Seamon is a fourteen-time grant recipient from cultural councils and recently celebrated her first solo museum exhibit in 2020. All of this culminated in her receiving the prestigious Albert Nelson Marquis Lifetime Achievement Award, for which she appeared in the *Wall Street Journal* in 2020.

She took a once-in-a-lifetime trip to Machu Picchu, Peru with the Punahou Alumni Association and her travel tale about that expedition is published in the 2021 September/October edition of the *Writers and Readers' Magazine*. Additionally, her Peru photography is the editorial feature in the 2021 fall edition of *DRIFT Travel* magazine.

Her horror short story, *A Cereus Curse*, is published in Terror Tract's *Hell-o-Ween 2021* anthology. Kira has never met a story from Greek mythology she didn't love and has kept a daily journal since her teens. *Dead Cereus* is her first novel.

CONNECT WITH LINKS:

Website: http://www.deadcereus.com
Facebook: Author Kira Seamon | https://www.facebook.com/authorkiraseamon/
Twitter: @KiraSeamon | https://twitter.com/KiraSeamon
IG: @authorkiraseamon | https://www.instagram.com/authorkiraseamon/
TikTok: https://www.tiktok.com/@authorkiraseamon

CAPTIVATING CARROT CAKE

FROM THE NIGHT LIGHTS BALL GALA DINNER

Ingredients

Cake:

- 4 eggs
- 1 ¼ cups vegetable oil
- 2 cups white sugar
- 2 teaspoons vanilla extract
- 3 cups all-purpose flour
- 2 teaspoons baking soda
- 2 teaspoons baking powder
- ½ teaspoon salt
- 2 teaspoons ground cinnamon
- 2 cups grated carrots
- 1 cup chopped pecans

Frosting:

- ½ cup butter, softened
- 8 ounces cream cheese, softened

- 2 cups confectioners' sugar
- 1 teaspoon vanilla extract
- 1 cup chopped pecans

Directions

Step 1: Preheat oven to 350 º F (175 º C). Grease and flour a 9x13 inch pan.

Step 2: In a large bowl, beat together eggs, oil, white sugar, and 2 teaspoons vanilla. Mix in flour, baking soda, baking powder, salt, and cinnamon. Stir in carrots. Fold in pecans. Pour into prepared pan.

Step 3: Bake in the preheated oven for 40 to 50 minutes or until a toothpick inserted into the center of the cake comes out clean. Let cool in the pan for 10 minutes, then turn out onto a wire rack and cool completely.

Step 4: To make frosting: In a medium bowl, combine butter, cream cheese, confectioners' sugar, and 1 teaspoon vanilla. Beat until the mixture is smooth and creamy. Stir in chopped pecans. Frost the cooled cake.

https://www.allrecipes.com/recipe/7402/carrot-cake-iii/

CLASSY CHICKEN CURRY

FROM THE NIGHT LIGHTS BALL GALA
DINNER

Ingredients

- 2 tablespoons. extra-virgin olive oil
- 1 medium yellow onion, chopped
- 2 pounds boneless skinless chicken breasts, cut into 1" pieces
- 3 cloves garlic, minced
- 1 tablespoon minced ginger
- 1 ½. teaspoons paprika
- 1 ½. teaspoons ground turmeric
- 1 ½. teaspoons ground coriander
- 1 teaspoons ground cumin
- 1 can crushed tomatoes (15-ounce)
- 1 ½. cups low-sodium chicken broth
- ½ cups heavy cream
- Kosher salt
- Freshly ground black pepper
- Basmati rice or naan bread for serving
- 1 tablespoon freshly chopped cilantro, for garnish

Directions

Step 1: In a large pot over medium-high heat, heat oil. Add onion and cook until soft, 5 minutes. Add chicken and sear until no pink remains, 5 minutes. Stir in garlic and ginger and cook until fragrant, 1 minute.

Step 2: Add spices and cook until very fragrant, 1 minute. Add tomatoes and broth and bring to a simmer. Stir in heavy cream and season with salt and pepper. Simmer until chicken pieces are cooked through and tender, about 15 to 20 minutes.

Step 3: Serve over rice or with naan, garnished with cilantro.

https://www.delish.com/cooking/recipe-ideas/recipes/a54696/easy-indian-chicken-curry-recipe/

GENUINE GINGER SNAP COOKIES

FROM THE NIGHT LIGHTS BALL GALA DINNER

Ingredients

- 2 ½ cups all-purpose flour
- 2 teaspoons baking soda
- ½ teaspoon kosher salt
- 12 tablespoons unsalted butter
- 2 tablespoons ground ginger
- 1 teaspoon ground cinnamon
- ¼ teaspoon ground cloves
- ¼ teaspoon black pepper
- Pinch cayenne pepper
- 1 ¼ cups dark brown sugar, packed
- ¼ cup unsulphured molasses
- 2 tablespoon finely grated fresh ginger
- 1 large egg, plus 1 egg yolk
- ½ cup granulated sugar

Directions

Step 1: Set the oven rack to the center position. Preheat to 300º F (149ºC).

Step 2: Line three baking sheets with parchment paper.

Step 3: In a medium bowl, whisk together flour, baking soda, and salt.

Step 4: In a 10-inch skillet (do not use nonstick, or you won't be able to see the browning), heat butter over medium heat. Once melted, reduce the heat to medium-low, swirl the skillet frequently until the butter solids begin to brown, about 4 to 5 minutes.

Step 5: Quickly transfer the browned butter to a large bowl.

Step 6: Add ground ginger, cinnamon, cloves, black pepper, and cayenne to the butter, whisk to combine. Cool slightly for 2 minutes.

Step 7: Add brown sugar, molasses, and fresh ginger to the butter mixture, whisk to combine.

Step 8: Add egg plus egg yolk, whisk to combine.

Step 9: Add flour to butter mixture and stir with a spatula until just combined.

Step 10: Tightly cover and refrigerate the dough until firm, 45 to 60 minutes.

Step 11: Roll the cookie dough into 2 teaspoon-sized (12g) balls, about 1 inch in size.

Step 12: Add granulated sugar into a shallow bowl and roll the cookies in sugar to coat.

Step 13: Evenly space the cookies 2 inches apart, about 20 per cookie sheet.

Step 14: Bake 1 sheet at a time until the edges are just beginning to darken, 20 to 22 minutes, rotating halfway through baking.

Step 15: Transfer the cookies still sitting on the parchment paper to a wire rack to cool completely. The cookies will harden more as they cool.

Notes

•Store gingersnap cookies at room temperature in an airtight container for up to 7 days.
•Freeze for up to one month, and then defrost before eating.
•Recipe adapted from America's Test Kitchen's *The Perfect Cookie.*

https://www.jessicagavin.com/gingersnap-cookies/

PURPLE YAMS

FROM THE NIGHT LIGHTS BALL GALA
DINNER

Ingredients

- 1½ pounds Okinawan sweet potatoes
- 2½ tablespoons unsalted butter
- ¼ cup half and half
- 1¼ teaspoons sea salt
- Freshly ground black pepper to taste

Directions

Step 1: Fill a medium-sized stock pot with cold water. Peel the potatoes and cut them into large chunks (approximately 2- to 3-inch chunks). Add them to the pot with the water as you go.
Step 2: Place the pot over high heat and bring to a boil. Reduce to low and simmer, uncovered, until the potatoes are tender (they should easily slide off fork prongs), about 15 minutes.
Step 3: Strain the potatoes and place them in a medium to large mixing bowl. Use a large fork or potato masher to mash them. (They can be as smooth or as chunky as you'd like.)
Step 4: Add the butter as soon as possible so that it melts into

the hot potatoes. Then add the half and half, salt and pepper, and mix only until everything is incorporated. Serve! (You can substitute orange sweet potatoes if desired or Yukon Gold potatoes for an even more buttery taste.)

https://cookingontheweekends.com/mashed-okinawan-sweet-potatoes/

SASSY SAUERKRAUT

FROM THE NIGHT LIGHTS BALL GALA DINNER

Ingredients

- 2 ½ pounds head of cabbage
- 3 ¾ teaspoons to 5 teaspoons salt
- (or about 1 1/2 to 2 teaspoons per pound of cabbage)

Directions

Step 1: Weigh your cabbage to see how much salt you should use.

Step 2: Remove the outer leaves of your cabbage and any that are damaged. Discard. Cut out the core and rinse the cabbage well, allowing the water to flow between the cabbage leaves. Drain well.

Step 3: Reserve 1 outer leaf. Thinly shred the remaining cabbage with a knife or food processor. Place in a large bowl. Sprinkle the calculated amount of salt over the cabbage and toss well. Let sit for 15 minutes.

Step 4: Massage the cabbage with your hands for 5 minutes.

The cabbage should release a good amount of liquid during this time.

Step 5: Pack the cabbage firmly into a very clean glass quart jar. Pour the liquid that was released during kneading on top. Cut a circle the same diameter as your jar out of the reserved cabbage leaf. Place it on top of the packed-down cabbage. Place a weight on top of the cabbage to ensure that it stays under the brine. If the brine doesn't completely cover the cabbage and weight, top off with a 2% solution of salt water (1 teaspoon salt per cup of water).

Step 6: Screw a plastic lid onto the jar. Place the jar in a rimmed pan (to catch any overflow) and allow fermenting at room temperature until the kraut is as sour as you like it. This can take anywhere from 1–4 weeks.

Step 7: After it's done fermenting, store the sauerkraut in the refrigerator.

https://www.thepioneerwoman.com/food-cooking/recipes/a100555/how-to-make-sauerkraut/

HOLLY'S RADIANT RASPBERRY MUFFINS

FROM THE MORNING GLORY DONORS EVENT

Ingredients

- 1 ¾. cups all-purpose flour
- 2 teaspoons baking powder
- ⅓ cup shortening
- 1 cup sugar
- 2 eggs, lightly beaten
- ½ cup milk
- 1 teaspoon vanilla extract
- 1 to 2 cups fresh or frozen raspberries
- Additional sugar

Directions

Step 1: Combine flour and baking powder; set aside.
Step 2: In a large bowl, cream shortening and sugar. Add eggs; mix well.
Step 3: Combine milk and vanilla; add to creamed mixture alternately with flour mixture.
Step 4: Fold in the raspberries.

Step 5: Fill greased or paper-lined muffin cups two-thirds full.
Step 6: Sprinkle with sugar.
Step 7: Bake at 375° F for 20–25 minutes or until center of muffin springs back when lightly touched.

https://www.tasteofhome.com/recipes/raspberry-muffins/

BRAISED RED CABBAGE THAT'S
WORTH THE WAIT IN LINE

Ingredients

- ¼cup (1/2 stick) butter
- 1 2-pound head of red cabbage, quartered, cored, very thinly sliced (about 14 cups)
- ½teaspoon (or more) salt
- 3 tablespoons dry red wine or hard cider
- 1 tablespoon red wine vinegar or apple cider vinegar

Directions

Step 1: Melt butter in a heavy large pot over medium heat.
Step 2: Add sliced cabbage and 1/2 teaspoon salt; stir and toss constantly until cabbage begins to wilt, about 7 minutes.
Step 3: Add red wine or hard cider and sauté until liquid evaporates, about 10 minutes.
Step 4: Add red wine vinegar or apple cider vinegar; stir constantly until cabbage is tender and turns bright fuchsia color, about 13 minutes longer.

Step 5: Season to taste with pepper and more salt, if desired. (Can be prepared 1 day ahead. Cool slightly. Cover and refrigerate. Rewarm, stirring over medium heat, before serving.)

https://www.epicurious.com/recipes/food/views/braised-red-cabbage-231603

GRILLED PACIFIC RIM TUNA

FROM THE NIGHT LIGHTS BALL GALA DINNER

(PAIRED WITH THE PURPLE YAMS)

Ingredients

- ¼cup low sodium soy sauce
- ¼cup fresh lime juice
- 1 tablespoon dried crushed red pepper
- 2tablespoons sweet rice wine
- 1tablespoons dark sesame oil
- 1 tablespoon grated fresh ginger
- 1 garlic clove, minced
- 6 (4-ounce) tuna steaks (1 inch thick)
- Garnish: fresh cilantro sprigs

Directions

Step 1: Combine first 7 ingredients in a large Ziploc® freezer bag; add fish.
Step 2: Seal bag and chill for 15 minutes, turning occasionally.
Step 3: Remove fish from marinade, reserving marinade.

Step 4: Grill, covered with grill lid over medium heat 5 to 6 minutes on each side or until fish flakes easily when tested with a fork, basting twice with reserved marinade.
Step 5: Remove fish to a serving platter.
Step 6: Garnish with shredded coconut if desired.

Yield: 6 servings

https://www.kingwood.com/recipes

SCINTILLATING SPAETZLE

FROM THE NIGHT LIGHTS BALL GALA DINNER

Ingredients

- 4 cups all-purpose flour
- 2 teaspoons salt
- 8 large eggs
- ¾cup milk

Directions

Step 1: In a bowl, whisk together the flour, eggs, milk, and salt. Stir until the batter is well combined and develops bubbles. You can also use a mixer. The batter should neither be too thin nor too thick, or it will be difficult to make the spaetzle with your spaetzle maker. Let the batter sit for 5–10 minutes.

Step 2: Put a colander into a bowl to drain the spaetzle once cooked and bring a large pot of water over high heat to a boil, add about 1 tablespoon of salt to the water, and reduce temperature to a simmer.

Step 3: Press batter through a spaetzle maker, a large-holed sieve, or colander into the simmering water.

Step 4: Work in batches. After using about 1/3 of the batter, stop adding new spaetzle and let them cook for about 2–3 minutes, or until they float to the top. Stir occasionally. Use a slotted spoon to transfer the spaetzle to the colander so the excess water can drip off.

Step 5: Serve the spaetzle immediately or sauté them in butter to crisp them up a little. If you don't serve or sauté them right away, add 1 or 2 tablespoons of butter to the hot spaetzle to prevent them from sticking together.

https://platedcravings.com/authentic-easy-german-spaetzle-recipe/

HOLLY'S WORLD FAMOUS RATATOUILLE

Ingredients

- 1 medium eggplant, cut into bite-sized pieces
- Kosher salt and freshly ground black pepper
- 3 tablespoons olive oil, divided
- 1 medium white onion, peeled and cut into bite-sized pieces
- 6 cloves garlic, peeled and roughly chopped
- 2 bell peppers, cored and cut into bite-sized pieces
- 2 large zucchinis, cut into bite-sized pieces
- 2 pints fresh cherry or grape tomatoes
- 2 tablespoons finely chopped fresh basil leaves
- ¼teaspoon crushed red pepper flakes
- 1 bay leaf
- 1 large sprig fresh rosemary *(or 2 sprigs fresh thyme)*
- ½cup dry white wine* *(or dry red wine)*

Directions

Step 1: Add diced eggplant to a colander and toss with 1 teaspoon salt. Let sit for 15 minutes, then rinse and squeeze out excess liquid.

Step 2: Meanwhile, in a large Dutch oven or stockpot, heat 1 tablespoon oil over medium. Add onion and sauté for 5 minutes, stirring occasionally. Add the remaining 2 table-spoons olive oil, garlic, bell peppers, and zucchini, and sauté for an additional 10 minutes, stirring occasionally, until the vegetables are mostly cooked through.

Step 3: Stir in the eggplant, tomatoes, basil, red pepper flakes, bay leaf, and rosemary, and cook for 10 more minutes, stirring occasionally. Slowly add in the wine, stirring the bottom of the pan to scrape up any brown bits that may have formed. Cook for 5 more minutes, stirring occasionally. Season with salt and black pepper and remove the bay leaf and rosemary.

Step 4: Serve warm with a side of crusty bread, quinoa, rice, or pasta. (I also recommend sprinkling on some Parmesan cheese, if you'd like.)

Notes

•If you do not cook with wine, feel free to substitute in 1/4 cup chicken or vegetable stock + 1/4 cup red wine vinegar instead of the wine.

•If you would like more of a stew consistency, feel free to reduce the heat to medium-low after 10 minutes, cover, and simmer for an additional 10–15 minutes.

https://www.gimmesomeoven.com/easy-ratatouille/

GLOSSARY OF NAMES

Glossary of Names

Ankur: Hindi name meaning "seedling."

Ashton Berkeley: (Ashton) English habitual surname transferred to unisex forename use, from the name of various places composed of Old English elements—*aesc* "ash tree" and *tun* "settlement," hence "ash tree settlement." (Berkeley) English habitual surname transferred to forename use, composed of the Old English elements *be(o)rc* "birch" and *leah* "clearing, meadow, pasture," hence "birch tree meadow."

Dahlia: A girl's name of Scandinavian origin, meaning "Dahl's flower." One of the flower names used occasionally in Britain (where it's pronounced DAY-lee-a). It seems to have recovered from what was perceived as a slightly affected "la-di-dah" air. The flower was named in honor of the pioneering Swedish botanist Andreas Dahl, which means dale. In the Victorian language of flowers, Dahlia denotes elegance and dignity.

Daisy: A girl's name of English origin, meaning "day's eye." Fresh, wholesome, and energetic, Daisy is one of the flower names that burst back into bloom after a century's hibernation. Daisy is now second only to Delilah among most popular girl names starting with D. Originally a nickname for Margaret (the French Marguerite is the word for the flower), Daisy comes from the phrase "day's eye" because it opens its petals at daybreak.

Daphne: Greek name meaning "laurel."

Drusus Dudley: (Drusus) Roman name meaning "oak." (Dudley) Anglicized form of Irish Gaelic name of *Dara*, meaning "oak."

Fabio: Meaning "bean grower," derived from the Roman clan name Fabius.

Heather: Named after the plant Heather, which are a variety of small shrubs with pink or white flowers that commonly grow in rocky areas.

Holly: English name derived from the evergreen shrub or tree.

Huckleberry: The name is taken from an Evergreen Plant that produces edible berries.

Ivy: The name Ivy is a girl's name of English origin. Ivy is derived from the name of the Ivy Plant, which got its name from the Old English word fig. . . . In the language of flowers, Ivy signifies faithfulness.

Jared: Jared is an English name meaning "rose."

Jasmine and Jessamine: The name Jasmine is a girl's name of Persian origin meaning "gift from God." Jasmine was derived from the Persian word *yasmin*, referring to the Jasmine Flower. Scented oil was made from the plant, and it was used as a perfume throughout the Persian Empire. Variants include Jazmin, Yasmin, Yasmine, and Jessamine.

Keifer: This boy's name is of Gaelic origin and means "cherished" or "pine tree."

Ogletree: The Ogletree surname is thought to be a habitational surname, taken on from the village Ochiltree (formerly

Uchletree), one of the oldest villages in East Ayrshire, Scotland.

Oliver: This name of English origin means the "olive tree" and symbolizes beauty and dignity.

Pomona: Roman name derived from Latin *pomus*, meaning "fruit tree." In mythology, this is the name of a goddess of fruit trees.

Rosemary: The name Rosemary is a girl's name of Latin origin meaning "dew of the sea, or Rosemary (herb)." The name derives from two Latin terms: *Ros* meaning "dew" and *Marinus* meaning "of the sea." The plant was termed "dew of the sea" due to its salty texture and its ability to thrive in coastal climes. Only after the Middle Ages did the English names of Rose and Mary become interchanged with the name Rosmarinus and give us the modern name we use today. In an ancient legend, Rosemary was draped around Aphrodite when she rose from the sea. **Snapdragon**: Derived from the Greek words *anti* meaning like and *rhin* meaning nose, antirrhinum, the Snapdragon's botanical name, is a fitting description of this snout-nosed flower. It's said that the common name for this colorful flower comes from the snap it makes when the sides of the "dragon mouth" are gently squeezed. While their actual origin is unknown, it's believed that Snapdragons were originally wildflowers in Spain and Italy.

Sweetpea: The scientific name of the Sweetpea Flower is Lathyrus Odoratus. It was derived from the Geek word *lathyros*, which means pulse or pea. *Odoratus*, on the other hand, is a Latin word that means fragrant. When it comes to floral language, the Sweetpea Flower is associated with delicate pleasure, blissful pleasure, departure, goodbye, thank you for the lovely time, and adieu. It's also well known that it is the birth flower of April.

Viola & Violet: The English word "violet" is taken from the Latin word "viola," which means "violet flower" or "violet color." Its full Latin name is *Viola Papilionacea*. Common Violet Flower meanings include innocence, everlasting love, modesty, spiritual wisdom, faithfulness, mysticism, and remembrance.

William: Dianthus Barbatus, commonly called Sweet William, typically grows 12–24" tall and features small flowers held in dense, flat-topped terminal clusters (3–5" wide). . . .

Genus name comes from the Greek words *dios* meaning divine and *anthos* meaning flower.

Wilton: English surname transferred to forename use, from the name of various places composed of Old English elements: *wilig* "willow" and *tun* "enclosure, settlement," hence "willow settlement." (Lennox) Scottish surname meaning "place of elms."

Sources: Wikipedia, Nameberry, babyname wizard, 20,000 names.com, Mccormick.com, Petalrepublic.com, Missouribotanicalgarden.org, Parenting.firstcry.ccom, Auntyflo.com, Florgeous.com Findanyanswer.com, Houseofnames.com

BIBLIOGRAPHY

RECIPES

Elliott, Tammy. *Carrot Cake III*. Allrecipes.com.

Foerster, Julia. *Easy German Spaetzle Recipe.*   Platedcravings.com: December 19, 2017.

Gavin, Jessica. *Gingersnap Cookies*.
    Jessicagavin.com: December 4th, 2019.

Handler, Rian. *Chicken Curry*. Delish.com: September 13, 2021.

Kastner, Erica. *How to Make Sauerkraut*.
    Thepioneerwoman.com: January 14th, 2019.

Wein, Valentina. *Mashed Okinawan Sweet Potato   Recipe*. Cookingontheweekends.com: January
    6, 2021.

GLOSSARY OF NAMES

Ankur: https://www.babynamemeaningz.com/Ankur-meaning-16805.

Dahlia: https://nameberry.com/babyname/Dahlia.

Daisy: https://nameberry.com/babyname/Daisy.

Daphne: https://en.wikipedia.org/wiki/Daphne.

Dudley: http://www.20000-names.com/tree_names_male.htm.

Fabio: https://www.sheknows.com/baby-names/name/fabio/.

Heather: https://en.wikipedia.org/wiki/Heather_(given_name).

Holly: https://findanyanswer.com/what-does-the-name-holly-mean-in-irish.

Ivy: https://nameberry.com/babyname/Ivy.

Jared: https://www.sheknows.com/baby-names/name/jarrod/.

Jasmine and Jessamine: https://nameberry.com/babyname/Jasmine.

Keifer: https://cafemom.com/parenting/plant-names-baby-names.

Ogletree: https://www.houseofnames.com/ogletree-history.

Oliver: https://www.sheknows.com/baby-names/name/oliver/.

Pomona: https://parenting.firstcry.com/articles/55-popular-roman-names-for-babies.

Rosemary: https://nameberry.com/babyname/Rosemary.

Sweetpea: https://www.auntyflo.com/flower-dictionary/sweetpea.

Viola and Violet: https://www.petalrepublic.com/violet-flower-meanings/.

William: https://www.missouribotanicalgarden.org/PlantFinder/PlantFinderDetails.aspx?kempercode=a573.

Wilton: http://www.20000-names.com/tree_names_male.htm.

CPSIA information can be obtained
at www.ICGtesting.com
Printed in the USA
FSHW011114050122
87402FS